A 200-year-old farmhouse with a stone
foundation is . . .

A WOMAN'S PLACE

"Sit on the doorstone, then, and listen."

"Listening, you can almost hear a clatter of
tools, a creak of harness. Human voices almost
mingle with the voice of water. Many feet have
stepped upon this doorstone; feet in moccasins,
booted feet, bare feet. You can almost feel their
passage; they almost brush your knee.

"The hillside is haunted. Wherever you glance
—seeing only bright leaves—memories stalk.
Ghosts move on the hillside; but they move
more quietly than deer.

"Sit on the doorstone, then, and listen."

As we listen, this tender story unfolds the struggles
and triumphs faced by five generations of women—
dreams of romance, a lost child, a wedding, a birth
and a death. A WOMAN'S PLACE is a haunting
and beautiful novel in which every woman will dis-
cover some par̶̶̶̶̶̶̶

A WOMAN'S PLACE

BY

ANNE ELIOT CROMPTON

Illustrated by Ted Lewin

BALLANTINE BOOKS • NEW YORK

Library of Congress Catalog Card Number: 78-598

ISBN 0-345-28790-8

This edition published by arrangement with
Atlantic-Little, Brown Books

Manufactured in the United States of America

First Ballantine Books Edition: June 1980

Contents

	Prelude	1
I.	The Ark: 1750	5
II.	The Web: 1800	45
III.	The Nest: 1850	91
IV.	The Cocoon: 1900	137
V.	The Summer Place: 1950	181
	Finale	218

Prelude

Even now water sings from the hill. Water still surges up through stony earth along an edge of impenetrable rock; and at this point on the hillside it bursts free. Water still rushes into light and flings out and down the rock-face into a stone bowl, hammered by a thousand years of water, falling.

With the first light of a cold spring morning the water shines pearl. Shining, it splashes down the hammered bowl to a small pool that gleams among dark rock-masses, and the darkness of great, thrusting pines. In the tallest pine a cardinal sings.

Tile pipe once channeled the water downhill at a northerly angle. Now the pipe is broken and scattered; and several streams search their own way down between rock and fern, along crumbling stone walls.

Curving over the hillside, lost in new forest, the stone walls meet and part like meandering streams. They mark overgrown pastures, forgotten fields. Wandering among fern and blueberry and juniper, they lead at last to the abandoned road.

The dirt road is lined with massive, sun-glinting

maples. On one side lilacs crowd the road; a few lilac seedlings actually grow *in* the road.

Untended for years, these lilacs bloom stubbornly. For many yards around them the air is rich with the scent of their heavy, purple blossoms; and with another scent which is subtle, vague as a dream, and cannot be quite defined.

The lilacs screen two cellar holes from the road. These cellars are built of hillside boulders, fitted and cemented with the builders' sweat. This cement has held. The larger cellar, facing the road, is easily a hundred years old. The smaller, an ell to the rear, may be much older. Its rocks are crumbling faster, a few have fallen in from the top. At its center a white birch glows pink in morning light.

Both cellar holes still show the ominous black tracks of fire; as does the immense maple looming in front. Fire once licked up the side of the maple; but new growth has almost healed that wound. Fire devoured the house that rested on these boulders; and no new growth has risen here but the shining birch. The birch arches into sunlight. It spreads its leaves and digs its toes into rubble, and cares nothing for the life it supplants.

This was certainly a mighty house. The hills of New England are pocked with cellar holes, homesites abandoned when the young moved west, or when taxes rose, or when new roads bypassed an area, and a village died. But few can boast the size, the sheer spread, of this ruin. This was a farm mansion, a tribal home. Great must have been its roaring fall, walls and floors and rooftree folding into the cellars. What a commotion tore the forest peace that day! (That is, if the forest had yet come creeping back through the high pastures.)

Come around to the back; sit down on the old back doorstone. It is bedrock, this doorstone. Its covering moss hides a secret, a message from eternity. Sit on the doorstone, then; and listen.

Birdsong rings through the woods. A breeze shakes the lilacs till they nod, dropping bright dew. High on the hillside the spring bubbles and murmurs.

Listening, you can almost hear a clatter of tools, a creak of harness. Human voices almost mingle with the voice of water. Many feet have stepped upon this doorstone; feet in moccasins, booted feet, bare feet. You can almost feel their passage; they almost brush your knee.

The hillside is haunted. Wherever you glance — seeing only bright leaves — memories stalk. Ghosts move on the hillside; but they move more quietly than deer.

Sit on the doorstone, then, and listen.

The Ark 1750

Who has found a valiant woman?
—*Holy Writ*

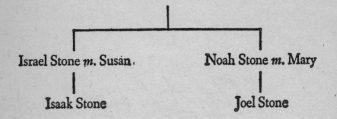

Israel Stone *m.* Susan.   Noah Stone *m.* Mary

Isaak Stone   Joel Stone

1

So tall stood the ancient trees they roofed the hills. Sunlight jeweled fungi clinging to their huge trunks, and mosses clustered at their feet. In a sea of ground pine and creeping jenny, fern islands fanned in rare pools of water-green light. Everywhere loomed rocks and boulders, flung and tumbled in a forgotten time. Touched by fingertips of light, they sparkled mica and garnet. Shadowed, the gray boulders slept like giant beasts. Through the high leaf-roof a constant wind sighed forever; and from every hillside gurgled falling water.

Through these hills wound a "military road" from Northampton to Albany. "'Tis no better than an Indian trail," Mary Stone would remark; and this, indeed, had been its origin.

A long day's journey from Northampton, Noah Stone drew rein. His brother Israel rode up beside him. The horses blew, shifted their tired weight, and rested in the wind-murmurous shade. Noah said, "Here. Here is the place."

Ahead, the trail ran along a plateau, then dipped

out of sight behind a clump of birches. To the right a rocky hill rose straight into the trees. Israel looked it over, glum and silent. To his farmer's eye, accustomed to flat, open space and accessible earth, their grant looked decidedly uninviting. Almost eagerly, with surprising enthusiasm, Noah pointed out its manifold beauties. For Noah had been here before; Israel was the newcomer.

"We can commence with those oaks; roll 'em down to the road, saw 'em on the bank. Build a slide here . . ." His vision expanded as he spoke. Noah's eye treated the existing scene as a limner treats an unsatisfactory canvas; mentally, he wiped out the wilderness, and repainted. Looking up the steep, boulder-strewn slope, he saw open fields advancing like armies over the decay of fallen trees; he saw scattered stones and rocks gathered into boundary walls; he saw cattle grazing in wide sunshine, flax and corn rippling in the breeze, his yet unborn children running barefoot; and to his ear the forest wind brought shouts, laughter, and the welcome clang of the dinner gong, rung from the doorstone.

Noah Stone was not young. Hardship and calamity had worked bitter lines about his dark, narrow eyes and compressed mouth. Mary Pettis, his second wife, had been his neighbor in another life, abruptly ended. Together they had left the settled community, which to them had become the place of death, and agreed to found a new life on Noah's King George's War grant. Noah sat his horse now, looking about on what Mary's relatives would call "that desolate wilderness"; and the vigor of determination rose in his veins, like sap in a blasted tree. Pointing up a near bank, he said to his brother, "My house will stand there."

"But you said there is a spring. Why not build by the spring?"

"Ayah, so I thought myself, until I found the site. I found" — Noah lowered his voice a notch, to reverence — "I found the site the Lord appointed to me."

"Eh?" Israel wrinkled his brow. The youngster brother, he looked the older. His brown hairline was receding so fast, he wore a town wig at all times; even here in the wilds.

"Ayah." Noah nodded gravely. "Come see." Dismounting, he hitched the horses to an overhanging branch — "The hitching stone will stand here" — and led Israel up the bank. On the first nearly level spot he stopped, hacked aside a spreading juniper bush, and scraped moss with his boot toe. "Look there." Israel bent, weathered hands on knees; gaped; and sighed astonishment.

The juniper overspread a huge, flat rock. Mosses softened its uncompromising lines; but it was sunk so deep in the bank it could never be moved, not with three oxteams in tandem. It was an unalterable part of the land.

Across its smooth, gray surface minced a series of marks. One would say that two small, three-toed feet, trotting across, had printed . . . cold rock? Israel licked his thumb and rubbed a print. It showed up clearer than before. He pushed a stubby forefinger into the next print. The tracks were graven in the rock.

Later, Mary would doubt Noah's explanation. It would strike her as a trifle too neat, leaving vast tracts of time and space out of account. But she would never try to argue it. Both instinct and cold intelligence warned her against argument.

To his dying day, Noah believed that this rock had once been a slab of mud. Did it not *look* like mud? Ergo! And while it was yet mud, Noah had let loose the dove from the ark. Over endless waters the dove beat weary wings. Here, momentarily, it rested. It crossed this mud with little quick dove-steps, then whirred up again into the watery wind.

And the Lord thought of Noah Stone, who would come to this place ages hence; ages which, to the Lord, were as a day. And He turned the printed mud into rock, a solid, lasting message for Noah Stone.

"Ayah," Mary would agree, pressing his callous-horned hand. Wisely, she would ponder her doubts in her own heart.

In this place, then, Noah raised his house, using the immovable rock as his doorstone. When Mary hinted about the spring, and easy water, he remarked that water ran downhill. "We can build a trough, even, carry water direct to your buttery! And look, you'll be close by the road, see the neighbors."

"Neighbors?" If Mary ever smiled, she would have smiled at that.

"Certainly, neighbors! Jacob Flower means to settle —"

"That jailbird!" Mary shuddered.

"And Squire Winter."

"Ah. Well." That sounded better.

"The Fiskes, the Cooks, maybe the Bennetts. We'll have a tavern here in the years, you'll see!"

Through the summer of 1750 the brothers worked on Noah's foundation. They sold their horses and bought oxen, small, but immensely powerful beasts with long, sweeping horns and kind eyes. So gentle were they, the ten-year-old cousins, Israel's Isaak and Noah's Joel, could handle them. They led the oxen, ran about hunting stones and branches for levers; and helped the women shovel out the foundation; while the Stone brothers bent their backs to war with rock, thus commencing a battle that would continue as long as the hillside was farmed. They dug and levered boulders out of the hill; rolled them down to the stone-boat, which the oxen hauled to the foundation; and swung them into place in the rising dry wall.

Israel's wife Susan was plump, blond and cheerful. She had left her four little girls with a relative until their house should be built; and she seemed to enjoy the freedom of this rough life. One night she looked up from the supper-fire, glanced around the exhausted group, and laughed. "We surely look a motley crew! We need not fear Indians — they would fear us!"

Susan was not overobservant. If Noah's dark face tightened, or Mary's hands trembled, she did not notice. And she was right, Mary thought, distractedly looking about the fire; they did look a sight! The men had loosened their britches at hip and knee. Israel had stored away his wig, and his bald pate shone frankly in the firelight. The boys looked as boys would always choose to look, did their mothers wink. She fingered the coarse stuff of her own homespun dress, ingrained with the dirt of weeks.

"As to that," she said to Susan, "shall we make holiday tomorrow? We'll go up to the spring and wash clothes. You men can all go bareback till we have done."

In the shadow of giant beeches the spring shone and twinkled, and cast silver light rippling across the white trunks. The water splashed down jagged rocks into a small pool. Susan jumped into the pool, fully dressed; delight spread over her simple face. Hopping about, she waved fat arms and shouted, "Cold! Wonderful! Wonderful!" She snatched off her cap, tossed it on the bank, and dunked her golden head under the fall. "Beautiful!"

Poised on a rock above the stream, Mary watched. The splashing waters, the brightness eddying on trees and rocks dazzled her. She felt as though she were leaning in a dark doorway, looking out into sunshine; admiring, desiring, but too weak to walk in the sunlight. Here was no place for her, she wanted to turn back into the dark, retreat to bed. Sorrow had no foothold here.

"Come on," Susan gurgled. "Waiting for something?"

Reluctantly, Mary stepped out of her cracked, patched moccasins. Hesitant, she dipped one grimy foot in the cold brightness. Susan laughed and tossed water in her face. Leaning away, Mary stumbled, and fell into the pool.

She entered a new element. She fell out of the dark doorway into sunlight, and it was shockingly cold, and it spoke and laughed all about her. She found footing and stood up, and her dress and hair hung heavy. She was shocked clear out of herself, and when Susan giggled, she giggled too; and presently they were laughing together, thigh-deep in the icy pool, dunking their husbands' shirts with the last soap, sending dirt downhill. Dirt and soap and habitual sorrow dribbled downhill together, as the pool cleared and brightened.

Panting, teeth chattering, they climbed out at last on the rocks and spread the clean clothes to dry on branches. Mary sat down, then, where sun struck through the leaf-roof and the rock glowed warm. She produced a comb, and they took turns tugging it through their water-matted hair. Dark and blond, lean and chunky, their reflections shimmered together down in the pool.

The comb dropped. Warming, they lay in the sun and listened to a woodpecker hammering back in the forest; and to shouts downhill, and the rasp and creak of the stoneboat.

Guiltily, Mary murmured, "We ought to be there."

Susan sighed happily, and spread her hair out around her to dry. "There's another on holiday," she said softly, glancing left.

Mary turned, quick enough to see Joel before he knew himself seen.

He stood in a pool of light, behind a fallen beech. Fungi like huge white moths perched along the trunk, half concealing the boy and the big black dog beside him. Boy and dog looked over the windfall, wary as wild things. Joel's hand rested on the big dog's neck.

This dog Noah called Balaam because, like Balaam's ass, it seemed to speak the King's English with its young master. It paid no heed to any other, but followed always at Joel's heel. And Joel, in turn, paid little heed to those around him, but caressed this dog, and watched it fondly, as a mother watches a toddling child. "He will outgrow it," Noah said. Mary was not so sure. She thought that shock had addled Joel's wits for good. She stepped around Joel, as she stepped around his dog, without expecting response; surprised if he noticed her presence. She cooked for him, washed and mended for him, and ignored him. His dumb-brute condition did not anger her, or even surprise her; for she felt its echo in her own heart.

He knew himself seen. He stepped back from the windfall. Like forest creatures, boy and dog faded into shadow.

"Tch-tch," Susan remarked. "That boy wanders a deal too much!"

But Mary sympathized. She knew the healing that could be found in solitude. She would herself like to wander, relaxing her heart. In spirit she went now with Joel; she scrambled among snaking roots, she chewed spruce gum. Under stiff, shiny leaves she sought bright-red wintergreen berries, eating as she picked them. She tore sheets of white bark from a paper birch, and rolled them to save under a rock, a secret treasure. "How do I know all this?" She wondered; and then remembered. Thus had her own small son wandered. One happy Sabbath she had followed him, and shared his delights.

"Mary," Susan warned, "You must not weep continually!"

"I?" Mary was startled, resentful. "I never weep!"

"Not in deed," Susan conceded, "but your look is always tearful. Not that I blame you! But you ought to show Noah a better cheer. He wants comfort, himself. As though he had not enough trouble, with that skulking lad on his hands!" Susan wiggled, turned on her side, seeking a softer couch. "To tell truth, Mary, I am glad Joel is not *my* stepson!"

2

On the last hoarded sheet of paper Mary wrote to her sister in Boston. "Young Joel is not yet reconciled. On the Sabbath he wanders the Woods, sometimes even on Work-Days. Sometimes he stays away till Dark, and this troubles me. For now the Days are short.

"The Cabin is ready for Winter. We have one Room over half the Cellar. My Husband has made a very handsome Chimney with Northampton Bricks, and a Granite Hearth, and now we cook withindoors. If You do not need Mother's Piggins, or the big Kettle, send me them."

From Noah's hearth a red glow flickered across the floor. At the round plank table Noah had knocked together Mary bent over her writing. A rushlight mounted on the flint box dimly lit the sprawling words. She wrote carefully but she was exhausted; her letters leaned wildly.

On their stringbed, Noah turned and resettled with much purposeful rustling. Israel and Susan, in the other bed, seemed to sleep. Only the tip of Israel's

14

nightcap peeked above their quilt. A ratlike rustle in
the loft betrayed the boys, spying down the hole.
Above them slanted a firm roof of heavy boughs.
"Noah has built a goodly House," Mary wrote thoughtfully, "firm; like an Ark."

The fireplace was the focus of the ark. The few pots
now hanging over the coals were battered, lusterless.
But Mary imagined her mother's kettle shining there,
cheerfully reflecting the glow. Suppose she fell heir to
her aunt's andirons! Once the relatives learned she had
a house to furnish, contributions would be in order.
She dipped her quill preparing to hint of this to her
sister; but refrained.

Instead she wrote slowly, with trembling letters,
"You in Boston may have Word of my Son before I
do. Let me know anything You hear, even Rumor."

Wind whined in the thatch. Mary called sharply,
"Isaak! Joel! Do not dawdle about in your nightshirts,
you will take cold!" A scampering rustle answered,
and a hopeful scratching at the door. Balaam, con-
demned to outer darkness, had heard his master's
name.

Mary rose, crossed to the built-in clothespress and
brought out her shawl. "Mary!" Noah whispered
loudly, "Do not dawdle about, you will take cold!"
Susan giggled.

"I will but finish this letter." Unsmiling, Mary
drew the shawl around her and sat down, reached
for the quill. Outside, wind rose.

Windy dark and chill opened a door in Mary's soul,
which in daylight she managed to hold shut. On such
a night as this the door swung open — as now — and
she stood helplessly looking at the thought, "Where
is David."

Images of David flashed through her mind, one
after another and back to the first, as on a whirring
wheel. Wrapped in a lousy blanket, David sat cross-
legged before a fire. Hideous, dark figures moved
about, Satan's henchmen. They did not frighten David

now; he smiled at them. He braided his hair, rubbed ash on his sweet young face, the better to mingle with them. This David was lost utterly to his mother, to his friends, even to God. Yet this was the most comforting of Mary's David-visions.

The next image was of David's corpse. It rotted beside an Indian trail, covered with ferns and fallen leaves. The back of its head was hammered flat.

Oh quick, quick, turn the wheel! There was David, again in firelight, but this time back in the cold shadows. This was no friend of the Savages, this was a slave. Emaciated, he trembled with a weariness he dared not admit, and watched hopefully for a bone, tossed from the feast.

Last appeared David, Frenchified. He knelt in a Papist church. Prayer beads swung, clinking, from his fingers. His round, pale face glowed rosy in stained-glass light; and heartfelt, heretical piety swam in his raised eyes. Across a sea of flickering candles, a jeweled idol regarded David tenderly. It clasped a wooden infant to its immaculate breast; and the infant held out tiny hands, and seemed about to crow and laugh. In all that false glow and flicker and shine, David felt warm and safe. He prayed to the idol in French.

Mary let the quill slide into the ink. Head bent on clasped hands, she prayed. Wind answered, rattling dry leaves against the ark wall.

Slowly Mary recovered. She raised her head, lifted the quill, and wrote with a determined hand: "Regarding Savages, there are none in these Parts. The Lord removed them from our path by means of Mohawks and Measles. We are blessed in this.

"Our Home is taking root. Do not trouble Yourself about the Piggins or the Kettle. But send me a sturdy Lilac Root from Your Dooryard. I think nothing would comfort and cheer me more.

"I love best the purple Lilacs, like those that shaded Mother's Door."

Noah went about the woods unarmed. He bound the blade of his King George bayonet to a wooden pole to use as a tool. His musket he laid away in the gun closet by the door, and his powder horn hung beside the fireplace. When the flame was high the figures scratched on the horn came to life: deer bounded from plug to tip; a bear bristled at a hunter; a savage crept up behind him, tomahawk in hand. Noah was no limner, but these crude drawings were his journal, the record of his life, or of a good part of it. Mary wondered that no children were depicted — Noah had had four besides Joel — and no woman. Only enemies and beasts were recorded, and the inscription "Noah Stone His Horne."

One rainy autumn day, while wiping soot from the chimney, she lifted the horn down, turned it, and came face to face with horror.

A rectangle gave off sunrays.

Mary dropped her cleaning rag. Hands and eyes glued to the drawing, she stood in a stupor. From the back of her mind sounded roarings. Mental tombs

17

opened. Fiends war-danced in earthquake. She no longer saw the horn she held, or the drawing. She saw flames. Then two small, brown hands came before her and lifted the horn away. She breathed, "David?" and swung around. "Joel."

His dark hair was rain-plastered. Waterfalls ran from the fringes of his vest. He looked down at the drawing, then back to her face; and in his dumb-animal eyes she saw recognition. "Poor child," her mind said, dutifully, "how can I help him?" But her heart was silent.

Joel hung the horn back on the nail, facing the burning house brickward. He opened his mouth with effort, and said in his flat strained voice, "My father wants the meal." Back in the open doorway Balaam whined. Joel flashed his hand at the dog, and it sat down to wait.

Mary said, "I thought . . . I thought . . ." Re-collecting her shattered mind occupied a long moment. "I thought they would come back for dinner."

Joel shook his head, scattering raindrops, and held out his hand. Probably the men had a fire going in a rock shelter. Mary filled a pouch with cornmeal from the chest and put it in Joel's small, hard hands. She watched him bound away through the rain, Balaam frisking like a huge pup at his heels.

After the rain came wind and hardening cold, then a black frost. Snow powdered the ground. And in this snowdust, wandering Joel came across tracks. He pounded back downhill, calling his father; "Sir! Sir!" Near-excitement brightened his face. Noah, Israel and Isaak were splitting logs for the Northampton trade. Noah paused long enough to climb the slope with Joel. Almost eagerly, Joel pointed. "Deer."

Noah squatted, peered, grunted. "Right enough. But mighty small. Ain't worth tracking." And he hauled Joel back to work by one red ear.

But the small deer did not need tracking. Appar-ently fascinated by men and their doings, it hung about. Noah, wiping sweat from his eyes, would notice a gray motion among gray trees, a flicker of white. Mary, climbing to the spring, would glimpse a stealthy shadow stalking alongside. And Joel in his roaming was often startled by a barking sneeze, and a white flash of tail soaring over a windfall. Balaam would tremble and growl, and perhaps pursue a short way. But very soon he would come trotting back to Joel's side. Nothing could tempt him far away from Joel.

One warm, bright day Mary and Susan went laundering again at the spring; and the whole time, the little deer watched from a distance, like a timid dog. Glancing back, Mary saw it peering from behind an oak-trunk. Its long, slender neck stretched around the trunk. It twitched leaf-shaped ears and snuffed; and once it stamped, as though to startle the women.

"It's almost like a pet."

Susan snorted. "When I was a little girl we had a pet pig."

"A pet pig!" The idea was delightful, ridiculous. "How long did you keep it?"

"Through the summer, naturally. Then we ate it."

Early one dark, cold morning Noah lifted his musket from the gun closet, took down the powder horn and stole out into the dawn wind. Mary, stirring up the last hasty pudding, heard the shot. Noah hung the deer in the exposed, unfinished half of the cellar. "Mighty spare," he said, cleaning the musket, "But we may be glad of it. Scraping the bottom, eh, Mary?"

"Nearly."

"That's what I thought. Time we load for North-hampton."

In brightening orange morning light the boys ran after the oxen. High up near the spring the humped brown backs moved among trees and stumps. The creatures foraged farther and higher as autumn advanced. "They'll clear some for us," Noah remarked happily. He was never so pleased as when he saw himself cleverly fending, gleaning prosperity in unlikely fields. "Two birds with one stone" was a maxim with him. "And they're fat enough," he added, watching the beasts bumble slowly downhill, prodded by the shouting children. Beside him, Mary marveled. She never ceased to wonder at the kind stupidity of the oxen, which could so easily turn, toss the boys into the brush, and go back to browsing. The notion never seemed to enter their dim brains. The oxen crashed through frozen ferns, trampled saplings, and emerged on the cleared slope, half trotting, half sliding down to the road. There, the boys loaded each beast to look like a horned, walking woodpile.

"We should be back in three days," Noah said. "You want meal, beans, molasses, tea. And what else might your ladyships desire?"

Susan cried, "News!" Mary handed him the letter to her sister. He stuffed it into his tobacco pouch, "Not to forget it!"

Noah had buttoned his britches, he wore proper boots, and carried musket and horn. Israel had on his town wig. To Mary's eye they looked elegant; but she knew that on the Northampton street they would appear rustic, rough; and that was no cause for shame.

Isaak looked up from struggling with tack. "Sir. Joel and I would like to go."

"Indeed," Israel assured him, "you shall, one day."

"Sir — "

Mary nearly intervened. For Joel to wish anything was surely a sign of health; the smoldering wick should not be quenched.

But Noah said, "We can hardly leave the women alone now, Isaak. You two dress the deer in the cellar, and carry wood and water." And that was the end of it.

Noah said the parting prayer. Standing in a close circle the group bowed its collective head as he solemnly intoned, "May the Lord watch between us, while we are parted from one another." And they were off, each man leading his ox, which moved like a burdened ship in a gale. The wood shifted and creaked and tipped threateningly with each ponderous step. "Did you ever see the like!" Susan laughed tremulously. Then she whipped off her apron and flapped it at Israel, who paused on the edge of the downturn to wave.

Mary said, "I wonder how long till we have a proper wagon road!"

Silence moved in. As soon as the travelers vanished, the woods seemed to stand up and shout silence. In fresh morning stillness the trees shone, pillars holding up the sky. Sunlight drenched the forest floor, now that the leaves were down. Close to the cabin were the raw marks of habitation: felled trees, charred stumps, gashed earth. But all around waited the untouched forest; bright, cold, silent.

"Listen, Sue; you can hear the spring!"

Susan nodded. Far and high, the bubbling fall of water teased the silence. For a quick, shamed moment, Susan and Mary held hands.

The children made holiday. Blithely ignoring wood, water and the undressed deer, they wandered off with Balaam into the cold forest. That morning they picked acorns, shining brown nuts which Mary wrapped in cloth and submerged in the spring to de-bitter.

"You can make a meal out of acorns," she told the children. "I know the . . . the . . ."

She could not say it, but Isaak could. "The savages do."

"Ayah. But that's hardly reason we shouldn't do likewise." Looking up, she met Joel's gaze. It was like looking into an animal's eyes. She was startled when he spoke.

"We can gather more. Another quartern, if you like."

"Why, yes. That would be provident." Was intelligence waking behind those blank eyes?

But in the afternoon the boys spied a coon high in a beech crotch, spitting down at them. Acorns were forgotten. They spent the short, fast-graying hours trying to bring it down with sticks, stones and foxy tricks. Balaam, watching, finally yawned and lay down. "Even the dog knew better!" Susan scolded. In the early darkness a light snow began to fall.

"We are for it!" Susan announced cheerfully. "This is only the beginning!" She piled wood on the fire — "There's plenty, Mary, look not so dour!" — and hauled both string-beds over by the hearth. "Look how cozy, we can all sleep in the warm! You lads take that bed, we'll have this one."

At Joel's plea, Susan Soft-Heart actually let Balaam indoors. He went immediately and leaped upon the boy's bed, nestling his bulk between them. "Oh, the dirty paws!" cried Mary, disgusted. Susan patted her hand. " 'Tis bitter out there, Mary. At least we can be cheerful together, withindoors."

Through the long night snow drifted between the cracks in the walls, and piled in fuzzy lines across the floor. The wind sighed and roared, lashing high, bare branches. Often Mary rose to feed the fire and pull the boys' quilt back over all of them; Joel had a way of drawing it close about himself. Toward morning she dozed, deeply enough to dream.

She walked down a field path, between stone walls splashed with little wild roses. The cows on the opposing hill looked smaller than the roses. Green heat shimmered around her, she squinted from under the grateful bonnet-shade. She held her apron folded, piled with dewy lettuce from a neighbor's garden.

Coming to a turn in the path, she knew that her own house was around the turn. In a moment its chimney would peek above the roses. Yet she had to go on around the bend, humming as she walked, shading the lettuce in her apron as though it mattered.

The chimney still stood. She saw it above the roses; black above the roses.

Lettuces dropped and bounced. Mary ran. About the foot of the black chimney smoked the ruins. Solo-

mon Pettis lay slumped against the gate. His shirt was
oily brown down the front, his head smashed in. She
looked once into his filmed, wide-open eyes; then she
jumped across his legs and ran into the ruins, screaming for David.

Uproar. Mary wondered, confusedly. The neighbors
had not yelled like that, they had come quietly, fear-
ing ambush. But here in the dark were yelling and
struggling, and a dog rumbling like thunder.

"Mary! Mary!" Susan shook her shoulder.

"Sue?" Mary lay stiff, horror-frozen. Shadows
played above her; fire-reflections on the ceiling.

"Mary, I'm here!" And Susan was there, warm and
enveloping, blowing sour breath down into Mary's
face.

"No roses. No roses. We'll have lilacs."

Susan hesitated, taken aback. " 'Tis nothing," she
said across Mary, to the other bed, " 'Tis a dream of
flowers!" And to Mary, "Surely, naturally. Lilacs."
She drew the tossed quilt back up, and went to sleep
with her comforting arm heavy on Mary's stomach.

They woke at the usual time. Gray light should be
slanting between the shutters. The cabin was completely dark, and bitterly cold. "One might as well be
out of doors," Susan declared, "and in one's shift!
Come; the men need never know, the preacher neither. We'll breakfast in bed!" And so they did, sitting
up with quilts about their shoulders. Mary brought
cold biscuits and tea to each bed, and cautioned Joel
not to share his with Balaam. She felt very queer and
guilty, eating and drinking in bed, with a lousy dog
in the next bed! "Unusual circumstances," she told
herself, unconvinced.

"Aunt Mary," Isaak asked, "could we have another
biscuit each?"

"No."

"We're hungry," Joel brought out.

"I could take another biscuit," Susan put in. "Would
it tax supplies overmuch?"

"Yes."

"Why! How low *are* supplies?"

"We have none."

"None?" Susan flopped around, astonished.

"None but half a quartern of acorns, up in the spring; a small deer, undressed; one sizing of Indian bread; and the sourdough." (The last, not to be eaten. It must leaven the next baking.)

Susan stared. The children looked at one another, then shrugged the quilt higher, till only their tousled hair showed. Joel whispered, "How do we feed Balaam?"

When Mary went to go out, she found the door blocked by more than a foot of snow, glowing blue in gray light. And still snow fell, piling softly, remorselessly. Staring from bed, Susan and the boys could see no farther through the door than that curtain of blowing, drifting snow.

"Jumping Jezebel!" Isaak murmured wickedly. "I doubt I can even get up to the spring!"

Mary ignored the profanity. "I doubt it, myself. We will melt snow for water."

It requires a powerful lot of snow to make a kettleful of water. The boys were very busy indeed bringing in wood and snow, and butchering the little deer. This messy work they performed in the open cellar, stumbling about in thigh-deep snow, turning their ankles on buried stones and stepping into postholes. Mary and Susan wanted to help, but masculine pride asserted itself.

"You go in the house, Mama, Aunt Mary," Isaak ordered gallantly. "This is men's work." He sawed valiantly at a haunch which Joel held taut.

" 'Pon my word, Mary, I think he's right!" Susan had gone green. "I never could stand pig day."

"This will never do!" Mary scolded primly. "You must not faint-heart now, Sue, when we must make do for ourselves!" But she pushed Susan up the ladder to ground level, and climbed up herself. They stood on top of the stone foundation, shaking out their snowy skirts and panting. Susan wondered, "What's wrong with the dog?"

Balaam faced the forest. His back was to the women, and they saw his hackles raised into a furry mane. He growled menace, all his muscles jerked and quivered. Susan shrilled "Joel! Call your dog!" Mary peered into the blowing snow, trying to see what the dog saw.

"Must be something out there," she murmured. "Speak softer." Snow whispered on snow. Nearby trees were vague, misty shadows.

Susan paled. "Might be a bear!"

"It might, indeed."

"The children!"

"They have Balaam."

Joel came to the foundation wall below them. He whistled to Balaam. The dog turned his head but continued to growl and tremble.

"Whistle again, Joel," Mary said. "You must keep Balaam with you in the cellar." She waited until Joel had coaxed the reluctant beast down, before shepherding Susan into the cabin.

"Perhaps," she soothed, "the dog smelled something far away."

"I have heard tell that a dog may know when its master is injured, or . . . dead."

Mary laughed without humor. "Balaam's master is out in the cellar, far from dead! Now Sue, shall we clean house?"

Susan glanced around the dark cabin. Firelight half lit the gloom. The two beds beside the hearth were tumbled silhouettes. Snow blew, rustling, across the floor. Susan shivered. "The broom is yours, Mary, with my blessing. But I am going to bed." And she did. Huddled in bed, wrapped in shawls and nightcap, she hugged her plump knees and droned; and later, hummed. Presently she called to Mary, who was sweeping snow out the door, "Mary, do you sing?"

Mary paused. Sing. *Sing?* "At Meeting," she answered finally, and shut the door.

Susan looked back over her shoulder. Her face had cleared, brightened a little. Some thought had lifted her out of fear. "We courted at Singing School," she said, "Israel and I. Every Tuesday and Thursday night. We would watch each other across the room, you know, and then we'd walk home together. Israel said I sang like a lark." Susan blushed.

Mary could see the scene, the schoolhouse lit by tapers; the fresh, pink faces lined up, girls on one side, young men on the other; and meaningful glances cast between, floating on sweet notes.

"Sue," she said earnestly, *"now* is the time to sing like a lark!"

" 'Tis what I was thinking. Listen, could the children learn this song?" And Susan lifted a clear, true voice.

> *He bids the sun cut short his race*
> *And wintry days appear.*
> *His hoary frost, His fleecy snow*
> *Descend and clothe the ground;*
> *The liquid streams refuse to flow*
> *In icy fetters bound.*

"That sounds good, Mama!" Isaak waved a ragged red haunch in the doorway. Joel and Balaam crowded in behind him. "This is all we could do right off. We'll go back later for the rest, but we were thinking if we could have this now . . ."

"Dear lad!" cried Susan, springing from bed. "Bring it here to the fire this moment!"

In short order the lean, stringy haunch was spitted over the fire, with a drip pan to catch any fat that might possibly fall; and cross-legged on their bed, the

children wagged their heads and swayed to the
rhythm of another song.

> *The old man he came home one night*
> *As drunk as he could be;*
> *He spied a horse within the stall*
> *Where his horse ought to be.*
> *My good wife, my dear wife,*
> *Oh wife so dear to me,*
> *Whose horse is that within the stall*
> *Where my horse ought to be?*

Mary protested. "You never sang that in Singing
School, Sue!"

Susan laughed and tossed her head. Mary thought
the rich smell of roasting meat had addled her wits.
"You are right, Mary, we never did! We used to sing
this at home — and softly, I assure you!"

> *You old fool, you durned fool,*
> *You doddering fool, says she;*
> *'Tis nothing but a brindled cow*
> *My uncle sent to me!*
> *The old man he came home one night*
> *As drunk as he could be;*
> *He spied a hat upon the rack*
> *Where his hat ought to be . . .*

Isaak joined in. The two voices rose loud in the
small room; the rooftree rang. Firelight reddened their
faces. Susan turned the spit, her hands trembling with
eagerness. Anxiety was wiped clean off her face,
only hope and brave merriment now shone in her eyes.

But Mary heard, over the ribald song, the whisper
of constant snow. She noticed when the wind rose and
branches creaked in the forest. Early dusk looked in
the cracks.

"Only another few turns," Susan announced. "Time

for another verse." She lifted her determined voice;
and now Joel joined in, droning a monotonous alto.

> *Whose face is that between the sheets*
> *Where no face ought to be?*
> *You old fool, you durned fool,*
> *You doddering fool, says she;*
> *'Tis nothing but a little lamb*
> *My uncle sent to me!*

Wind and dark; a sick unease in Mary's stomach.
Quietly she drew her shawl close, and let herself out
the door.

Blinded by stinging snow, she hugged cruel memories, drew them close about her like the shawl. If
only, if only there were *three* little boys singing at the
glowing hearth! She fancied David's small arms about
her neck. She pressed him, squeezed him to her heart.
But strangely, when he lifted his face he was Joel.

Closing her eyes, she prayed. "Save him from the
enemy's power, save him from his pursuers. Smile on
Thy servant, once more . . ." A burst of laughter from
the cabin roused her. She opened her eyes; bent to lift
her skirt out of snow; and saw at her feet a dent in the
soft, new snow.

Blurred, indistinct, fast filling in, the dent was un-
mistakably a human footprint.

Mary gasped, and leaned against the door.

A moment gone — even as she opened the door to
come out — a human being had passed. And this
human being, who must be the only one from Albany
to Northampton — this person had not knocked, had
not asked or offered help. He had simply walked past
the door — Mary whirled, looking for the next track.
There it was, and the next, they followed the wall to
the corner, and ended.

A moment gone, a person had walked around the
corner and down the ladder. He had small feet and a

short, pigeon-toed stride. He wore moccasins. "Lord
let it be David! Deliver him in Thy mercy, Lord!"

Very, very quietly Mary slipped withindoors, and
lifted from the gun closet the bayonet-pole. It was possible she might be mistaken, though her heart thudded
hard certainty. It was possible, too, that David might
not know her. He might be afraid. Why had he not
knocked?

It was dark by the door, the others did not notice.
They bobbed and bowed and waved excited hands,
black against the red light. The dog sat on the bed between the children, head cocked, sniffing the beautiful
odor. The stringbed creaked and groaned as the boys
bounced.

Very, very softly Mary went out, holding the bayonet stiffly before her, business end out. She was breathing hard, and sweating. Joyfully, her heart drummed
her ribs. She followed the vanishing footₓrints to the
corner.

"Oh Lord . . . Oh Lord . . ." She poked the
trembling bayonet around the corner, and leaned
around after it.

Snow blew in her face. The cellar was nearly dark,
a study in misty and solid grays. For a breathless moment she saw nothing. Her eyes swept the area eagerly, then frantically. "Lord . . ."

He moved.

By the hanging carcass an arm reached up; a small,
thin arm in a fringed deerskin sleeve. The childish
hand held a knife; and as Mary watched, it sliced a
hunk from the carcass, and lowered. His back to
Mary, the boy stood by the carcass. He seemed a little
older than David; but naturally, David had grown.
Moving clear of the corner, Mary stood on the foundation and watched as he cut down hunk after hunk of
meat, and bent to stow them in some bag or pouch, at
his feet. When he bent, a stiff black braid stuck up
over his shoulder. Once he paused in his work, glanced
left and right; but not back, over his shoulder.

If he had looked back, he would have seen Mary. She stood in full view, shawl rippling, bayonet still trembling. Slowly she lowered the weapon, for joy rushed from her heart down her arms; and she could hardly hold the foolish thing, for trembling. She was half aware of silence from the cabin. Herself, she stood in a cocoon of silence. Her heartbeat seemed suspended. A minute, now, and he would turn and see her. He would run into her arms. But let it be a long minute, this heavenly wait; let it last forever!

David straightened, and looked apprehensively toward the cabin. Song burst forth within, this time a sacred song, sweetly intoned. Gone was the dull, underlying drone. Joel was singing the tune.

> *There is a land of pure delight*
> *Where saints immortal reign;*
> *Eternal day excludes the night*
> *And pleasures banish pain.*

David bent again to his work. Squatting, he stowed the last meat in his bag; only, it was not a bag. Mary saw now, it was a blanket; for he had to roll the meat in it, and hoist it over his thin shoulder. He came to his feet in one graceful motion, and gave the clean, swinging skeleton a last inspection. Satisfied then, he turned around.

Why did he have to steal, Mary wondered, the thought too quick for words. Why did he not knock on the door and say, "I am David Pettis escaped from the savages, and I am hungry?" Was the poor lad that shamed? She took a step forward. On the edge of the foundation, she opened her arms to him. The bayonet hung, unnoticed, from one half-frozen fist.

David looked up. He gasped. She heard the intaken breath, saw his mouth drop darkly open. He stiffened, head high, like a startled wild creature. Mary whispered, "Sweeting . . ."

But he was not David.

She must have known it all along, somewhere underneath, for she recovered instantly. Strength surged back into her arms, the bayonet came up, resolutely aimed, unshaking. She looked along the steady blade into a small, round face. The dark, veiled eyes looked up at her from another world. It was his gaze, more than his dimly discerned features, that told her he was not David. He was child of no relative, no friend of hers, he came from utterly beyond. Fierce, bold and baleful, this child's gaze was that of a dangerous man. And Mary, looking into his startled eyes, watching him gather himself for an effort, knew with final certainty that her David was not alive. Etched in the flying snow between herself and the boy she saw the most grievous of her visions: David's corpse, rotting under leaves, under snow.

The child darted quick glances at the surrounding stone walls. If he dropped the stolen meat he could easily scramble out the other side of the cellar. And this was Mary's wish. "Go!" She rasped at him, finding shocked voice, "Go that way to the Devil!" Ashamed and perplexed, she realized she did not want to hurt him. He was only a little older than . . . "I'll call the dog," she warned. Actually, she knew she would not be heard above the singing. The voices in there were strong and true as a singing school. Real music floated out to the cellar.

> *There everlasting spring abides*
> *And never-fading flowers;*
> *Death, like a narrow sea, divides*
> *This heavenly land from ours.*

Mary saw the child make up his mind. He knotted the ends of the blanket firmly about his wrist, and strode toward the ladder, and Mary. Near he came, pacing softly like a catamount, fixing her with his alien

gaze. The bayonet commenced to shake as the child
advanced upon it. He paced a stately stride nearer,
and now the point was at his breast. His hand reached
out — a small, square hand, like David's — and
gripped the blade.

It was the hand of a little boy. The face behind
the hand was a child's face. Not the braided hair,
nor the strange, different smell, not even the ferocity
of his expression could alter that. The little hand laid
the blade firmly aside. A moment the boy looked up,
assessing Mary with somber eyes, breathing in her
face. Then he laid hand on the ladder, and climbed
up beside her. He brushed against her. One foot trod
on her skirt, lightly, as though a cat stepped there.
Holding her gaze with his, he edged past.

> *Behind fields beyond the swelling flood*
> *Stand dressed in living green;*
> *So to the Jews fair Canaan stood*
> *While Jordan rolled between.*

Mary turned to face the boy. Still facing her, he
walked backwards. Still gripping his blanketful of
stolen meat he backed off, with his free hand he drew
his knife and showed it to her, as a retreating animal
might bare its teeth. And so watchful, defensive, he
withdrew like a shadow into blowing snow, and vanished.

Mary leaned against the wall. The bayonet dropped,
resting its clean point in the snow. She had met a
savage. She had smelled his wildness, he had trod on
her dress. Somewhere in this stormy dark the child
trotted, confident, needing no love, guidance or provi-
sion. He had provided excellently well for himself!
It was too dark now to see the dangling skeleton, but
Mary knew it was scraped bare. From Albany to
Northampton, there was nothing now but a triumphant
Indian boy running, loping through ever-deepening
snow.

"That is, unless there's a camp of them. If that boy goes back to camp with this meat and tells them where it came from . . ."

Weakly, Mary sat down in the snow.

4

Susan said, "I thought I heard wolves last night!"

"So you did," Mary told her calmly. "They kept me awake." She had indeed tossed and turned, listening to the wolf-song from the hill; but it was not this that kept her awake. Another dread entirely kept her listening, watching the ember-reflections on the wall; and several times she rose to listen out the door, staring into snow-stinging blackness.

She had told them nothing. No need, she thought, to frighten Susan; poor, good Susan taught the children songs and cat's cradles, told them stories. More should not be asked of her. And Joel; what shock might shine in his eyes, did she mention savages to him!

Besides, she was mortally ashamed.

She said, "An animal took the meat." It was her first lie. She thought it was justified; and not entirely a lie.

"The bear!" Susan cried. "That's what the dog told us! Only think, how close it came!" Mary observed her terror with affectionate scorn.

The children looked up, both faces alive with excitement. "Bear! We must have a trap!" That kept them happily busy all morning. They explored the clearing, hunting for "sign"; they dragged a log out of the woods and constructed a flimsy deadfall on the foundation. "He might come back for the bones."

Susan was fearful for them; but she said, "So long as you have Balaam with you. And look around!"

"Ayah," Mary agreed. "Call if you see anything. *Anything.*"

Every half hour she fetched her shawl and patrolled the clearing, glancing sharply into the forest and along the military road. She half expected to glimpse dark forms humping between the snow-walled trees, brandishing knives and tomahawks.

"Are you ill, Mary? You go out so often."

"I like to walk in the storm."

Susan stayed in bed, climbing out occasionally to feed the fire. "I've about run out of songs," she told Mary in the afternoon. "Can you not remember one song, Mary, only one song to sing tonight?"

But Mary knew no music. Song, like laughter, eluded her.

Slowly her fear gave way to hunger. Walking the clearing, she weakened. Her legs shook, and she had to push herself to take each step. In the afternoon the children came in, dumped their soaked clothes to dry on the hearth, and climbed into bed. Their eyes looked hugely out of small faces, gone dead-white. Balaam jumped into his now-accustomed place between them, turned about twice, and settled down with his head on Joel's knee.

Isaak piped, "Aunt Mary! What can we feed Balaam?" Balaam thumped his tail across Isaak's feet.

Susan said, "Balaam is better off than we. Look how chunky!"

Joel spoke. His disused voice grated like a millstone. "I think we should all sit in bed and wait. That way, we need not eat."

Mary said, "A good idea. We might also pray." Prayer was a thing Mary knew. She taught them prayers, as Susan had taught them songs. Through the short evening, prayers went up Noah's chimney with the smoke.

Late at night Mary crept to the door and looked out. "Dream," she thought, and lightly slapped her cheek. The great trees stood clear around the cabin. Their branches fingered milky sky. Their blue shadows rippled across the clearing to Mary's feet. Caught in an elm-fork, the full moon hung like a lantern.

Mary looked back into the cabin. After the clear, moonlit air, the cabin smelled stuffy. Susan writhed. The children moaned. None of them was conscious, yet they did not sleep. Restless hunger kept them fidgeting.

She glanced back at the snow-blanket. How long would it take two men and two oxen to wade home from Northampton?

Gathering up her skirts, she stepped into the snow. It flowed thigh-deep. Even the Indians whom her terror imagined camped nearby, might find the going difficult. Fearful of stalking shadows, she examined the landscape. Only tree-shadows laced the snow. In the corner of her eye, that hulking form —

She lurched around; and recognized the boys' deadfall.

For a long, freezing moment she stood shaking, regarding the deadfall. And a thought that had been growing slowly in her mind, a seed in dark earth, abruptly bloomed.

Never before had she called the dog. They had had no commerce together. Uncertainly she whispered its name as she stole indoors, and took the bayonet once again from the gun closet. "Balaam! Balaam!" And a little louder, "Balaam!" Almost prepared to give up the scheme if the animal failed to respond. It was a harebrained scheme. It would demand strength, and more courage than she felt.

The stringbed creaked. Paws padded across the floor. Stealthily, as though it shared her wish to let the others sleep, the big dog came to her side.

She led him out to the moonlight, pushed the door shut. He looked up at her, curious, with moon-glinting eyes strangely resembling Joel's.

"Come," Mary whispered diffidently, "This way, dog. Come, Balaam." And she began to wade strenuously along the wall, where she had walked so joyfully the night before. The dog followed, dubious. Its head hung, its drooping tail swept the snow.

At the corner she stopped. "Go on," she told the dog. She gestured to it, as to a human companion. "Go on." Miraculously, it seemed to understand.

It swam past her, its broad black breast cleaving the snow, and stood on the foundation, looking down into the cellar. The deadfall shadowed its back.

Mary plunged her hands in the snow, found the trigger, and pulled. The log fell.

She was amazed that the trap worked at all. But in falling, it did not finish the matter. The dog's back was not broken. The log had merely pinned the animal down in deep snow. Mary, working furiously with bayonet, stones and bare hands, had to complete the task.

She needed the rest of the night to scrape and tug off the heavy skin, and chop up the carcass. The moon was sinking, and gray dawn slinking among gray trees when she dumped the dog chunks into the kettle and poked up the fire. She had considered several methods of concealment. She could burn the skin, throw clean snow over the blood, raise the deadfall, fill in tracks. But in the end, Joel would know. Grimly, she left the evidence in sight. Let him hate her if he chose.

Witchlike, she crouched on the hearthstone, gloating. A wonderful smell presently rose with the steam; and behind her, the beds creaked.

"Mary," Susan mumbled, "do I smell cooking?"

"You're not dreaming, Sue."

Proudly, Mary dished up dog soup. Susan and Isaak sat up in bed, slurped greedily, asked no questions. Joel went outside.

Bowl in hand, Mary watched from the doorway. Joel followed the tracks to the corner — her tracks, and the marks of paws and sweeping tail. There he stood, looking. Long he looked; and when he turned and saw Mary, his gaze was as alien as that of the Indian lad.

While Isaak chopped and hauled, Joel passed the day in bed. Dumbly he gazed into the fire. Emanations flowed from his small hunched form. Passing near, Mary was washed by waves of hate. Angered, she thought, "What does he think I should have done? Let us all starve for his mangy cur?" So she talked herself back into courage, and met Joel's hateful stare with equanimity.

In the evening Joel gave in, and sipped a bowl of soup. "Now he cannot hate me anymore," Mary hoped. But now the emanations swirling about him were deeper, colder. Now he hated himself.

Another short, frigid day they lived thus. All about the cabin the snow sparkled, silver at noon, blue and rose at evening. The immense tree trunks shone green and orange. Evergreens sighed and rustled, lacing the snow with purple shadows. Within the cabin, Mary and Susan wrought order, a return to dignity. They swept and dusted, and trimmed the rushlights; they set the beds back in place and spread the quilts. Finally they sat by the hearthstone waiting, listening. Outside sounded ax and saw, Isaak's laughter, Joel's grunts.

Mary asked, "Was it only two days ago that Joel sang?"

"Do not fret, Mary. He has made a beginning. He will sing again."

"I would like to hear him speak!" She coddled a bowl of soup, sipping it slowly. Fed and warm, in an ordered room, she could think. Probing in her mind, she tried a door; gingerly. The door swung open and she was looking at grief. But that was all, now, only grief. The monster Hope was laid.

"Susan. Sue, how much did Joel see of . . . of his home, after . . ."

"Why, he saw it all." Susan looked across the hearthstone at Mary, surprise clear on her honest face. "Did you not know?"

"I never asked."

"Oh? Well, Joel had been at our house. He came to ask Israel to look at a sick cow — milk fever, I think it was. Well, Israel went back with him, and there they saw, you know, dead youngsters on the doorstone — "

Mary thrust out a silencing hand. "And Joel saw it all, the way I did?"

"Aye."

One thing more. "And was the dog with him, then?"

"Let me see. Must have been. Ayah, must have been."

"Oh, Sue!"

"Mary not now! Not yet! You must not!"

Through gathering tears, Mary saw alarm in Susan's eyes. "You are right." She blinked. "I had forgot." Despite warmth and a food supply, they were not yet safe.

Safety came home the following day. Safety came on snowshoes, leading the exhausted, laden oxen. In silence the two boys at the chopping block watched the approach. When the men waved, the boys waved back. There were no shouts, no calls or jubilations. Yet the women withindoors sensed a difference. They came out in the knee-deep snow, lifting stiff skirts, shading their eyes. Blue shadows came humping awkwardly along the military road. The snow-glint rendered them almost invisible; but the squeak and crunch of snowshoes neared, and an ox groaned.

Mary closed her eyes against the glare. Behind the lids, bright tears welled and swam.

5

They ate meat pies and biscuit, pudding and apple-molasses. They drank toddy. They sat like Christians at the table, and ate from trenchers; and Mary set a ewer of water in the middle for cleansing greasy fingers. All the pots were full all day; and in the evening Mary and Susan strung dried squashes and apples, and the boys hung them from the beams.

Noah had packed a swift in his load, an hourglass, candles. Candlelit, the cabin took on a prosperous glow. Susan sighed happily. "I did not think to live Christian again!"

"Susan sang," Mary told the men. "She taught the children."

Israel grinned. "Singing School did us no harm!"

Noah said little. Tired, he sat by the fire, powder horn in hand. He turned it around, examining the drawings; then drew his knife. The scrape of steel on horn accompanied Susan and Israel's songs till bedtime.

Mary watched Joel. While Isaak nodded and waved to the music, Joel sat frozen. More than ever now, he reminded her of a dumb beast. She would have gone to him, touched his shoulder; but she feared he would bare his teeth.

Alone indoors next morning, Mary dared to lift the powder horn down and turn it, searching. She shuddered at the burning house; but it was no longer too much for her. She passed on, rolling the horn on her palm; and came to a new drawing.

For the first time, Noah had etched a woman's figure. She stood soldier-straight, facing a bristling dog.

Mary hung the horn back on the chimney, and took up her broom; and slowly, as she swept, began to smile.

Through the winter Joel remained frozen. Mary found herself fretting over him. She searched for opportunities to touch him: "Joel, come help me clear browse for the oxen." "Joel, come with me to the spring; these buckets are heavy." "Joel, help me scour these pots. They need a strong arm." Willingly he bent his back. But his eyes never met hers.

Then in the first spring softening, when from every hillside ran rivers of melting snow, when wild geese flew over like northward-aimed arrows, and pussy willows fuzzed, Noah and Israel returned to Northampton. This time their sons went with them. Joel almost thawed. He seemed nearly happy at the prospect of travel. He brought Mary his britches to mend. He patched his moccasins, and combed his hair differently. Noah said, "I think if he stayed home this time, he would forget the King's English." He was joking; but she nodded seriously. This trip might wake Joel. Nothing she could do had worked.

With Susan, she waved off the convoy. Oxen, men and boys tramped away down the military road, disappearing immediately behind a screen of new, furled leaves. Mary and Susan went back to their garden, a sunny, rocky patch of earth beside the cabin.

Digging up stubborn roots with Noah's bayonet, Mary rambled on about the lilac bush she hoped her sister would send. Where should it grow? Not by the door, where the heedless men would trample it; not beside the cabin, where Noah hoped to build an addition. "I think, Sue, I'll put it down beside the road."

Susan was thinking more about her own home, whose four corners Israel had staked before leaving. "My roses will go beside the well," she decided, "where the little ones can water them." Susan was eagerly waiting to see her four little girls again. She had had enough of freedom.

On a later morning, young leaves cast delicate shadows across the cabin walls. Birds twittered and swooped, partridges drummed from the hill; and Mary was on her knees, very carefully sprinkling turnip seed, when Susan screamed.

Mary leaped up, seeds spilling down her apron. Susan grabbed up her skirts in both hands and galloped toward the road. "Emmy!" She yelled. "Polly! Nessie! Lamb!"

Mary relaxed, wiped her grimy hands on her apron, and stepped down the bank with dignity.

Little white bonnets flashed through the leaves. Four small, exhausted children fell into Susan's arms. She knelt in the road, hugging, kissing, crying, her embrace gathering and spilling children. Mary looked over her head at the approaching men. She looked first at Noah; he waved his walking stick in salute; then at his son.

Hope surged in her heart. Joel did look different. His eyes held a trace of light. He walked straighter, looking ahead, instead of at his toes. He did not smile, or wave; but that would be asking too much.

They gathered in the road, and Noah said a brief

prayer of thanksgiving for a successful journey, happily concluded. Then Mary asked, "Noah, did my sister send . . ."

His blank look changed to one of sudden guilt. "Your sister sent you a package at my aunt's house."

"Let me see!"

"Well. It did not look then as it looks now."

"Noah, what *do* you mean?" She almost danced impatience.

"Well. It was wrapped in damp papers."

"Naturally!"

"But then, Mary, we had a long climb. Very hot." Noah wiped his neck, and dramatically showed her the soggy kerchief.

"Did you leave my lilac root behind?"

"No. Oh no. Well. Here it is." He handed her his walking stick.

It was, indeed, a lilac sapling. Two wilted leaves clung stubbornly to its top. Sadly, Israel handed her his cane. "And here's the other one."

" 'Pon my word!" Mary looked from one pathetic stick to the other, mumbling sorrow. "I don't know what to do with them!"

Joel edged between the men. "Aunt Mary, I'll plant them." Everyone but Susan, who was still volubly greeting her little ones, looked in amazement at Joel.

Mary managed to say, "I'd take that very kindly."

So it was Joel who dug two holes in the bank, lugged water down from the spring, and spread the pathetic, dried-up roots. He held the stems straight while Mary shoveled the loose, stony earth back around the roots. She watched his sturdy, brown hands patting the earth down.

"You have planted them so carefully, perhaps they will live."

He took up the bucket and shuffled uphill again. Mary called after him, "If you water them each day, they will surely live!"

Joel watered the lilacs. Through the summer they

sucked spring water into their wrecked, ragged roots. First one, then the other, put out tentative leaves. Beside the military road, on the cleared bank, they stood in full, gracious sunlight. Sunlight entered their leaves, moist earth-mysteries entered their roots; the lilacs lived. They grew, to cast delicate morning shadows on the bank, and dapple the stones at their feet with leafy shade.

Mary and Joel never became close. Theirs were not warm, forgiving souls. For thirty years more they shared the house, which grew only a little more slowly than the farm. Like the two lilacs, they stood side by side in stony soil, vigorous and self-contained, brushing each other lightly when a strong wind blew.

But at some time during those thirty years, perhaps while watching at a sickbed, or nooning during harvest, or popping corn on a winter evening — at some time, then, Mary did tell Joel the story of the Indian child.

The Web 1800

Fair as a star, when only one
Is shining in the sky.
—*Wordsworth*

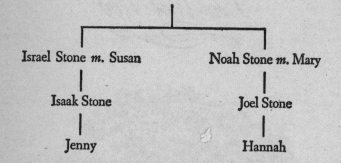

Israel Stone *m.* Susan   Noah Stone *m.* Mary

Isaak Stone   Joel Stone

Jenny   Hannah

𝒆❧ 1 ❧

Under dewy lilacs the young girl waited. Her faded blue dress blended with the purple blossoms that bowed and nodded about her. From any distance, she thought, she could hardly be seen, standing blue in purple shadow. But she did not realize how her apron flashed white, twisted in nervous hands. This might betray her presence to one looking out from the house, or down from the high fields.

Thin, eager, tense, she stooped slightly, head pushed forward ungracefully on her stringy neck. Long black hair, still in its night-braid, swung down her back. She twisted her apron, cocked her head, watched the bridle path. From the house behind her sounded clatterings and thuds. The door stood open to the spring morning, and the sounds of Delight's violent housekeeping carried to the path. Hannah twitched a smile. At least, Delight was not looking out at the lilacs!

From farther and higher came the faint blowing of horses and men's shouts, gentled by distance. A vast and cheerful peace breathed over Spring Hill, as morn-

ing sunlight slanted through the maples and elms lin-
ing the path. Chickadees hopped in the lilacs, shaking
down dew. Hannah leaned farther out, listening.

And now she heard the clop of approaching hoofs.
Her heart blocked her throat.

As the sound came clearer, closer, she withdrew
into the bushes. Her thin hand sought her mouth. It
might not be Caleb, after all. Another neighbor might
be riding past Spring Hill on his way to town. Suppose
it were old Cousin Isaak, for instance; what might he
think to see her standing here, ghost-white, with her
night-braid hanging!

Harder, faster, came the hoof beats. Cousin Isaak
did not push his nag like that! This was someone hur-
rying, someone young and excited. Just around the
bend the horse whinnied.

Golden bars of light fell across the path. At the
bend a halo framed the slight brown mare and
cloaked rider: Caleb. His red-curling hair caught the
sun as he punched the mare into a gallop.

Hannah skipped into the path, arms flung wide.
The mare swung aside and checked at the last instant;
simultaneously, Caleb was out of the saddle and Hannah in his arms.

She leaned against his chest as against an oak-
trunk, breathing in his leather-sweat odor. This was
also the familiar odor of her father, and of the hired
man, and usually she noticed it with faint distaste.
But from Caleb she welcomed hot odor, hard kiss.

Caleb raised his head at last, caught his breath,
and said, "Goodbye."

Hannah locked her hands at his back. "You did
not come to say that!"

"You know what I came to say. Wait for me. You
will?"

"Forever."

"It will hardly be that long. I should have a claim
staked by fall." They kissed again, clasping with sad

urgency. The mare ducked her head, snorted, pawed impatiently, rattling dirt and stones about their feet.

"Hitch her to the stone," Hannah murmured to Caleb's neck.

He glanced around at the hitching stone. It stood clear of the bushes, in plain view from the house.

"They'd see."

"Delight's in the kitchen — hear?" Delight's powerful voice swelled in song. "Praise God from Whom all blessin's flow," she shouted, and tossed out the dishwater.

" 'Tain't the old slavey I'm thinking of!"

"Father's in the high field."

Caleb pulled free of Hannah's arms, led the mare to the stone and passed the reins through its iron ring. Swinging back to Hannah he caught her again in his arms. The sun rose through the maples, and now the world was gold.

"Why," Caleb asked when he could speak, "is your father so dead set against me?"

" 'Tain't you he's against so much, 'tis your going away."

"He doesn't want to lose you, is that all?"

"He hasn't a peck of daughters, like Cousin Isaak!" And Hannah added softly, "If only you could agree to live here — "

Caleb shook his head violently against her cheek. "I'm going where there's a big sky. We've never seen a sky like where I'm going!" He drew away a little, gesturing passionately. "No stone walls out there! No humping hills! No cabins jammed full of brats! Out there we start fresh."

Hannah had heard all this before. Her imagination could hardly keep up with it. To her, only Caleb was real. His vision and his journey were but dreams. She followed when he pulled away and gripped his waist with thin but powerful arms.

"You must send me letters."

"I haven't set hand to paper since that summer Miss Fiske kept school, remember?"

She nodded, pressed against him.

"But I'll write you, soon as I've a thing to say."

"You won't forget!"

"You? No chance! And you promise to wait."

"I told you; forever." Hannah took Caleb's head in her work-rough hands. She stroked his bright hair, pinched his ears, pulled his mouth to her own. Dragging himself away, he untied the restless mare and swung into the saddle. Heels poised to kick, he hesitated.

"Hannah. Does your father want someone else for you?"

Hannah laughed.

Caleb tossed his head and kicked the mare, and passed away from Hannah in a shower of dust and pebbles. She was left looking after him, her defiant laugh frozen, like a grimace of grief.

A while she stood in the path, mentally riding pillion with Caleb. With him she crossed the brook, aware when the mare stumbled among the stones. She watched cows watching him over stone walls, and Goodwife Fiske waving to him from her doorstone. With him she ducked under low, blooming apple branches. Then the cleared fields and scattered cabins fell away. No stone walls followed the path farther, nor was it arched now by sugar maples or elms, casting friendly shade. The forest closed in.

As the brown mare entered the forest Hannah's soul sighed and slipped off the pillion and returned to the body that stood in the path. Unwilling, slow, that body turned, went through the gap in the low wall, and up the bank toward the house.

Foursquare, two-storied, the house presented an end to the path; for Joel Stone, Hannah's father, intended one day to build a wing across that end, facing the path. For now, the house had no dignified public face.

Unfinished, it sat on its granite cellar like a bump on
the hill; immovable, earth-rooted as God's mountain.

Gray as the enclosing stone walls the unpainted
boards blended with the hillside. Morning sun glinted
on the end facing east toward the path, and twinkled
the little window panes. Beyond, Spring Hill rose into
sunshine. Above the chimney smoke, Joel Stone and
the hired man plowed each his small, walled field.
They called cheerful taunts and challenges back and
forth, and their shouts echoed from the pasture across
the path. Behind each straining man and horse a wake
of new-turned earth shone, rich brown as the horses'
coats.

Flurrying a small flock of scratching chickens, Hannah turned the corner and went into shadow. The
door, with its carved lintel and worn, wide doorstone,
stood open. She passed quietly in, and turned right, to
the kitchen.

This kitchen was the original house. As a youngster,
Joel had lived here with his father and stepmother,
and sometimes his cousins; and he had built on the
living room gradually, and raised the roof, as his for-
tunes improved. To one coming in from sunshine the
kitchen seemed dark indeed. The beams, walls and
tables were of dark oak originally, and fifty years of
smoke had left them darker. The great fireplace was
soot-black. Black pots dangled from black cranes and
hooks. But the glow of the small, summer fire cheered
the room, brightening the flint box on the round, plank
table, the pewter dishes on the shelf, and two rag rugs,
braided by Hannah's mother. Near the window,
loom and spinning wheel were set up for work. The
floor was swept, dishes washed and shelved, and bread
dough rose in pans on the hearth. Delight's long day
was well begun.

"There you are," she cried, skipping in from the
buttery. "I was lookin' for you to skim and churn, 'tis
my bake day, did you forget?" Talking, she seized
the broom and swept, vigorously and unnecessarily.

Mouser, her gray cat, flowed through the buttery door and slithered among the bread pans.

Mouser was a concession hard-wrung from Joel Stone, who generally refused animals houseroom. (Hannah remembered begging hopelessly for a puppy.) By his silent toleration of Mouser he admitted Delight's indispensability. This — with the considerable food she consumed — was the old woman's pay. She slept on a pallet in the buttery, or in winter in the kitchen, under a quilt pieced from her old clothes. She worked endlessly.

"As for the young fellow, 'tis good riddance you know, sweet. Look at how he's gone off to the wilds of Ohio or some such with never a thought for his old mother and brothers — did you think yourself the only one left? Oh, no! And if he'll do that to his old mother, think what he might do to you, sweet, did you cast in your lot with him! 'Tain't that kind you want! Though what kind you do want, your father don't seem to understand, he don't!" And Delight cast her broom in the corner and burst into song.

> Oh! Lead me to the rock
> That's high above my head,
> And make the covert of Thy wings
> My shelter and my shade.

Hannah did not trouble herself to answer. Stiff with her secret, dark with youthful hostility, she went out to the buttery to skim and churn.

The small buttery was cool, ever shadowed. It was furnished with shelves of milk pans, the churn, Delight's pallet, and music, tranquil and eternal. For a wooden trough led through the west wall and out the south wall, and through this trough flowed clear spring water from the hill. In the middle of the room, purling water paused to deepen in a bucket. The little girl Hannah had loved to rest her chin on this bucket, and watch the water whirling gently around its wooden walls, eddying toward the top. She would scoop up a palmful to drink, less for thirst than for wonder. Hannah drank now, holding back her braid with one hand.

Later in the morning Hannah followed the trough up to the spring, and paused there to fill a bucket for the thirsty men and horses. Where the bright water welled and spilled, Grandfather Noah had built a springhouse, both to protect the spring from pollution and for cold-food storage. Hannah reached into the dark little house and drew out a cheese. For a moment she rested, watching the water slide, bubbling, down the trough. Then she hoisted her load of bread, cheese, oats and the water bucket, gathered her skirt up, and bumbled uphill.

Across a field she trudged, and over a stile into a mowing. As she balanced, swaying, atop the stile she heard her father shouting, above. His words did not carry, only the gladness in his mighty voice. She glanced up and saw him wave across the wall to the hired man. He had noticed her approach. He shouted to Ginger, his great chestnut gelding, and pulled back on the reins, digging in his heels. The hired man's horse, gentle Betsy, stopped at a word.

When Hannah reached the wall between their fields the men were sitting in the shade of a giant maple. Under the next maple the horses waited, flicking at flies, shaking their long, coarse manes. Man and beast looked hopefully to Hannah as she laid out the food on a flat stone. First filling the men's mugs, she carried the bucket to the horses. One by one — Ginger first — the heads dipped, the sober, dark eyes spoke, the soft muzzles slobbered.

"Enough!" Joel roared around a mouthful of bread, and Hannah had to lift the bucket away from the reaching horses. Apologizing, she patted each damp nose.

"Well!" Joel swallowed, and continued, "So young Cook rode off to Ohio at last! Here's one glad to see him gone." He thumped his sweat-stained chest. "Now maybe a girl can look around and see someone else, eh? Somebody better worth the seeing?"

Hannah felt her face hotter than before. She looked away from Joel. Her eyes met the hired man's.

Lott Flower was a small man, dark, very powerful. He spoke to the horses, to Dolly Cow, rarely to Joel. To Hannah, only his eyes spoke. They were like the horses' eyes, somber, direct. They sent Hannah a direct signal now, which she did not care to read. She flushed hotter, twisted her hands in her apron, looked out along the field. From here she could see the smoke from Cousin Isaak's chimney. The hillside was clear nearly to the top; and if Cousin Isaak were out plowing with his sons, she should be able to see them. She strained her eyes, looking.

Joel bantered on. "Cook lingered a while by yonder bush. Long enough to say a plenty of sweetness!" He wiped his mouth on his sleeve, leaned forward. "Listen, girl. I'm glad 'tain't *my* son gone to Ohio, for I'd likely never see him again. Ohio swallows young men like the grave. So, we who stay at home have to look after each other. See?" He nodded, smiling up at Hannah out of the dappled shade.

Looking down at him, she wondered at his smallness. Actually, Joel Stone was big, heavy-muscled. He ruled his house and all in it. He subdued the earth in true Biblical fashion, by his own sweat and the sweat of his shambling beasts. But Hannah saw him small beside the shadowed maple. She saw him soft beside the stone wall he had built. She saw him like a struggling ant beside the mountain he had tamed.

She looked down upon him from an exalted height. Determination lifted her above his schemes and hopes. She thought that he could no more bend her will than he could plow the sky.

2

Hannah's mother Emma lay in the graveyard under a granite slab. Leaf-shadows laced the slab, ferns embraced it. "EMMA," it read, "WIFE OF JOEL STONE D 1790 AE 32." A curt summation. But clasped hands were inscribed at the top of the stone, and the arching word "WELCOME."

Hannah wondered about those clasped hands. Was death truly like that? Did the invisible soul rise from bed and body to clasp an invisible, greeting hand? At Emma's dying, she had guessed at neither spirit. Joel had stood back from the bed, rigid and silent. Judging by his face, he had felt no passing spirit, either. Yet he had paid a field of flax to have those clasped hands inscribed.

"They're goin' in." Delight jostled Hannah's elbow, and nodded toward the meetinghouse. The doors stood open, the congregation was crowding into the dim, suffocating interior. Insistent bell-clangs sank down through the heat as stones sink down through water.

"I'll come." The old woman darted away to the door. But Hannah lingered.

Emma's stone was flanked by three smaller stones, inscribed: "JOEL STONE SON OF JOEL AND EMMA STONE"; ABNER"; and "INFANT." Joel and Abner had come and gone before Hannah's arrival. Infant had taken Emma with him. Hannah wondered about those four souls. Were they together in unimagined, breathless joy? Did they stand about a glassy sea, wearing golden crowns? Or had God tossed Infant into hell, casually, as Joel might toss a spoiled ear of corn into the fire, because he was unbaptized? The Reverend's God was monstrous cruel. Joel's God was unapproachable, like Joel himself. Hannah had once been young enough to asked Joel where Mama was. He had shrugged. "No way to know. Find out when you get there."

"Papa, where do you *think?*"

Joel heaved the saddle from Ginger's back to his shoulder, and trudged to the shed door, Hannah at his heels. Mouser ran out between his feet. This was the young Mouser, sleek and slender. In her mouth she gripped a golden chipmunk, limp, with shock-misted eyes. She zipped into the high grass. Joel nodded after her. "There you be," he said to Hannah. "There is no difference between man and beast. All go into one place. All are of the dust, and all turn to dust again. Now be off, girl, fetch me a mug of tea."

So quietly he said this, Hannah was not sure she had heard it aright. It did have a Scriptural sound; and later she heard Reverend Jones read it from the pulpit. This gloomy philosophy, and Mr. Jones's gloomier one, seemed at odds; and both were at odds with the bright confidence of Delight's hymns.

The bell pealed its last, the doors were closing. Within the meetinghouse sounded thunder: the hinged seats clattering back as the congregation rose for the invocation. Hannah straightened her bonnet, clutched her daisy-caraway bouquet between her tiny breasts, and stepped forward smartly.

The spinsters' pew was beside the door, the last

on the right side. Hannah slipped in beside Cousin Jenny Stone. Her tardiness went almost unnoticed, though beyond Jenny, Nancy Fiske and Eunice Little shot arch, suspicious glances. As for bubbly Cousin Jenny, she seized Hannah's hand and held it through the invocation, until with a mighty rumble the congregation seated itself. Then Hannah withdrew her hand and wiped it, under pretext of smoothing her skirt. Jenny's hot hand was almost slimy.

Jenny was prettily plump. Sunny ringlets cascaded free of her go-to-meeting bonnet. Despite the heat, her gingham was iron-fresh. Hannah wondered how she had ever reached the iron, with all her sisters clamoring for it!

Just behind the spinsters on the gallery stairs, the Stone children twitched and snuffled. All the children in town were there, on the stairs or in the gallery; and a high percentage of them were named Stone, Bennett, or Cook. Goodwives Stone and Bennett sat together in the second pew from the front. Across the aisle were Joel and Cousin Isaak, shoulder to broad shoulder; arms folded, they listened to Mr. Jones with fierce attention, for they were first in precedence after Squire Winter himself, and deeply conscious of the responsibility.

Jenny's attention soon wandered. Hannah felt her warm, moist breath near her cheek, coming and going as Jenny turned her pretty head forward, or sideways. At the first strains of Mr. Little's bass viol they stood for the hymn; and Hannah, glancing quickly at Jenny, saw that she was looking sideways at the bachelors' pew across the aisle.

"Be Thou O God Exalted High" echoed from the rafters; but Jenny faltered, singing two wrong notes. And when the seats rumbled down again and Mr. Jones began the discussion — "The laborer is worthy of his hire" — Jenny was still looking steadfastly sideways. Her breath fanned Hannah's cheek like a warm, rainy breeze. Later, when Mr. Jones's voice sank to a

drone like that of the droning flies, Hannah stole a
glance across the aisle.

Next to the aisle slumped Lott Flower. Eyes on the
floor, head drooping, he almost snored. Beyond him
— in Caleb's accustomed place — was Harry Bennett.

For the past seven years Harry had been appren-
ticed to a shoemaker in Northampton. Now he was
traveling the hill towns. Hannah wondered if he were
making shoes for the Bennetts; very likely, there
were plenty of growing feet in that house. But where
would he sleep? In the shed, like a hired man? Joel
referred to the Bennett household as "the rabbit run";
not without envy.

Harry leaned forward, elbows on knees, as though
entranced by the discussion. But his gaze was locked
with Jenny's. Sunshine filtering through the leaf-
laced window haloed his chestnut curls. His lower lip
drooped dreamily, revealing the absence of two front
teeth. His brown eyes and Jenny's blue ones relayed
a message so constant and intense as to tickle Hannah's nose in passing. Loneliness rose like a sudden
wave from the well of her mind and engulfed her.
Was Caleb sitting at this moment in a strange meetinghouse? Did they have such a thing in wild Ohio?
Why had he sent no word?

To one starving, the sight of others feasting is in-
tolerable. Hannah turned her gaze back to Mr. Jones's
pale, impassioned face. She tried to listen to his every
word. She drew her skirt away from contact with
Jenny's skirt; with her turkey-tail fan she swiped at
flies and at the message almost perceptibly winging
across her. She, like the enraptured pair, gave off a
powerful emanation; a mixture of scorn and envy that
amounted to hate. But Jenny, crushed confidently
against her, did not seem to feel it.

Toward the end of the discussion the heat in the
meetinghouse became truly overpowering. Goody
Fiske sank in a near-faint; and Mr. Jones called

intermission. Gratefully, the congregation wandered about the shady lawn, gathering in picnic groups under the maples. The children snatched a bite and ran off among the graves; no shouting was allowed, and each child had to keep its shoes on. Tied up and down the street in the shade of arching elms, the horses blew, munched in their feed bags, and swished at flies.

Hannah sat with Nancy and Eunice on a wild-strawberry bank. They peeled boiled eggs, and searched among the leaves for a few tiny, jewellike berries. Hannah made a sincere effort to follow the talk of ribbon, calico, and the price of peddler's trim. But her heart was stirred. Even as she nodded solemnly at Nancy's story of the young peddler, she thought about Caleb; about Jenny and Harry; and what God might be planning for herself.

Glancing away, she saw her father under the next maple, stooping to listen to a very pretty girl at his elbow, Jenny. Jenny cocked her head, tossed her ringlets, and beamed up at Joel, while beside her, Harry smiled and gaped. Joel turned to him. Shyly Harry held his ground, nodding affirmation. Joel looked back to Jenny and flashed his rare, dark smile. In a typical Jenny-gesture she seized his arm and squeezed — something Hannah would never dare do — and Joel went on smiling!

"Hanny, you haven't heard a word I've said." Nancy scrambled up, brushing leaves from her dress. "And now the application's due. Well, you'll just have to wait and see."

Wait and see what? Oh, the new dress. "I can't wait."

"Hah!"

Mr. Jones appeared on the meetinghouse steps, bell in hand. Picnics were gathered up, running children called; and the congregation, covertly sighing, filed back into the sweltering building.

Joel moved up beside Hannah. "Harry Bennett's coming home with us," he murmured.

"To stay?"

"Ayah."

Through the application, Hannah wondered. "I have two good pair. Delight makes her own moccasins. Papa's winter boots can maybe stand a mending . . . but enough to keep a shoemaker in the house? Whatever is he thinking of!"

ᏋᏄ 3 ᏒᏍ

So Harry Bennett whipped the cat at Joel Stone's. That is to say, he brought lathe, leather and awl, and plunked himself down on the hearthstone with Mouser. The extent of his visit should have depended on the number of shoes the Stones needed made or repaired. Harry put Joel's winter boots in order the first day. The second day he made Delight an unnecessary pair of new moccasins, and mended a gaping hole in her old ones. At supper that night, Joel looked around the table.

"You got shoes need mending, Hanny?"

"No, Papa, mine are still good." Hannah went barefoot much of the time. She saved one pair of shoes for heavy fieldwork, and the other for go-to-meeting. After a year of such wear, they were still quite new.

"How about a new pair?"

Hannah stared. "Papa, I have two pair!"

"Never yet heard of a girl refusing new clothes! Make her a pair, Harry."

That kept Harry busy two more days. Cunningly, he stretched it to four. By now Hannah was almost accustomed to the sight of him stooped by the fire, or on the doorstone, punching and sewing. He was a handsome, good-natured young man. His presence brightened the rather gloomy atmosphere of the house. But Hannah was not really aware of him. He was not Caleb.

He slept in the shed with the horses, Dolly Cow, and Lott Flower. Hannah watched curiously to see how Lott would react to this. Lott could hardly withdraw further into himself, or retreat deeper into resentful silence. Withdrawal and silence were his nature. But he took to going about slouching, watching his feet, and acknowledged orders with a shrug.

"Mark me," Delight warned Hannah at her churn, "Flower's going to blow like spoiled beer!"

Hannah nodded anxiously. She feared Lott's temper.

Hannah's new shoes made, no more excuse could be found for maintaining a shoemaker. Harry sighed, and packed his saddlebags. But, "Stay!" Joel urged. "It's come haying time." Harry stayed on as an extra hand. But he received no wages. He stayed for a different reason altogether.

The first day Harry set up shop on the hearthstone, Cousin Jenny came tripping over the hill path to borrow a quartern of butter. The day after next she returned the quartern, and showed Hannah the calico she had bought from Nancy's peddler. Should she make a full skirt or a skimpy dress? Which would Hannah advise? Hannah advised the full skirt; and

Jenny — an expert seamstress — had a surprising amount of trouble with this skirt. She sought a great deal of Hannah's help and advice. Hannah saw more of Jenny that July than during the whole of the past year.

Immersed in her own problems, she was slow to catch on. "Cousin Isaak's cow is better than ours. What can they want with our butter?" "Goodness, Jenny taught *me* the butterfly stitch the time we had mumps. What is the matter with her?"

Delight explained. "Make haste my beloved; be thou like to a roe, or to a young hart upon the mountains."

"Oh." Hannah stood on the doorstone and watched Jenny flouncing home up the hill path, hopping from hillock to hillock, very like a young hart upon the mountains. Harry stood on the springhouse, watching her go. He watched there, after she had passed from sight.

"Oh." Now she knew why Harry milked and weeded for free; but why Joel took any interest, she could not imagine.

One August morning Hannah and Delight toiled at the fireplace, stirring, cranking, shifting reflectors closer to the fire, or farther away. When noon light splashed the windows Delight went out on the doorstone to ring the dinner gong. Hannah darted upstairs and changed her sweat-soaked dress.

Gathered at the plank table the men watched approvingly as the heaped platters came off the hearth: new potatoes, string beans, tiny onions, thick slabs of cornbread, a bowl of butter, coffee. As the young men took up their knives, Joel folded his hands and looked up at the ceiling. "Bless this food, O Lord," he began, "and grant that the horses may not stumble; that Innkeeper Brown will give fair value without half a day's discourse; and that I may not have to wait another day in Northampton for the Post."

Hannah laid down the spoon she held ready. Her hand trembled.

Not another word was spoken until the plates were refilled and Delight poured coffee. Then Hannah asked, "Will you stay at Brown's, Papa?"

"Unless Cousin Thorpe invites me to stay."

Hannah wondered in passing how many new potatoes would pay for the night's lodging; but another matter lay much closer to her heart. "Papa, will you be fetching the Post?"

" 'Tis my turn."

"I . . . I . . . might have a letter. You wouldn't lose it, drop it, or . . ."

Joel barked laughter. "We might have snow tomorrow!"

"Truly, Papa. I might have a letter."

Joel drained his mug and pushed his plate away. "Nary a letter have I dropped or lost." He turned to Lott. "I'm ready when the horses are."

Lott was going to work on his third mug, but he swung promptly out of his chair. "Keep my coffee hot," he told Delight, "I'll be wanting it." He strode out the open door.

Hannah clasped nervous hands in her lap. "Lott's not going?"

"Got business to tend here." Joel shrugged. "Fact, I'm glad to leave a man at the house. Never know what may come up. And Harry here — he'll be busy tonight." Joel grinned at Harry, who looked down at his plate. "If you like," Joel told Hannah, "you can have Flower sleep in here." Hannah looked down at her wringing hands, and shook her head; hard.

Lott brought Ginger and Betsy plodding to the door. Both big, brown horses were already sweat-shiny, loaded from ears to tail with sacks of trade vegetables. Ginger led Betsy, and Joel took Ginger's lead rein. "See you tomorrow," he told his household, gathered on the doorstone, "unless the Post is late." He waved, tugged at Ginger's rein, and away they went, the two big horses, the big man, and the swaying mounds of vegetables. Gently they ambled down the dusty path, under the dappling, shifting shade of the great maples.

In the cool buttery Hannah washed the dinner dishes. Afterwards she took off her apron and sank down on Delight's pallet. Through the open kitchen door she glimpsed Delight's foot pumping the treadle of the spinning wheel. Delight hummed a hymn, the wheel hummed, water gurgled down the trough. Hannah curled down on the pallet for a minute's nap.

This evening, she thought, Papa will reach Brown's Inn, about six of the clock, when the light lengthens. He will go straight for the Post, of course; and they will hand him a sack of letters for Winterfield. Of course he will look through them to see where to stop off, coming home; and he will see one for Hannah Stone. He must! Surely, he will!

Certainty welled in her heart like spring water in the bucket. Higher, deeper, eddied the tide of sureness. And she smiled, picturing Joel's astonished face. "Snow in August!"

She tried to picture Caleb writing the letter, ever so many days gone. But this was too hard. She could not see where he sat, in the light of what lamp, or candle, or sun. But she saw clearly the words he wrote, the words she would read tomorrow. "I have staked out our farm. In the spring I will fetch you."

"Wait," purled the water. "Wait," hummed the wheel.

"Well I never," was Delight's comment, when Hannah woke toward evening. "I never heard of a strong young thing sleepin' like that in the middle of the day! Babies sleep like that, and sometimes youngsters will, though mostly they're runnin' faster'n you can watch 'em; and o' course *oldsters* like a nap now and then, specially after dinner. Now, an old woman might lie down like that at high noon and kind of doze off; leastwise, if she was on her own bed, and not in nobody's way that wanted to work."

Hannah took her grandfather Noah's bayonet, and went out back to the stone-walled garden. Noah had used this bayonet against French and Indians. Back in Noah's day there were still a few scattered Indians to be met in these hills: Nipmucs, Nonotucks, Norwattucks. But Noah went in no fear of them. When he came to Winterfield he was near middle age, and Hannah thought his disposition must have mellowed; for he removed this bayonet from his musket, lashed it to a broom handle, and thus in true Scriptural fashion, made a garden hoe. There could be no more effective weeder.

Weeds were few; but Hannah knew how fast they could grow. They could entirely choke the young carrots and onions in a week. Especially after a rain, their sturdy green fingers would come poking out of the earth like sins from an unrepentant heart. Attacking the one, she felt virtuous, as though rooting out the other. Strange, she thought later, how her mind dwelt, that evening, upon sin! While her back and arms wearied, a conviction of sin grew upon her. She worked while the light failed. When she could no longer distinguish weeds from carrots she straightened her sore back, and looked into Lott's face.

Lott Flower was not a large man. He was wiry-strong, rather than muscle-bunched, like Joel. But in the near dark, straddling a potato hill a yard away, he loomed sinister. Hannah gasped. She stepped back away from him, onto a carrot row. She glanced down, skipped off the carrots, and looked up in time to see Lott lunge.

Hannah's ordered, rigid mind could not accept what she saw. She saw the menacing shape of the man plunge toward her, she saw his hard hands grasping for her, heard his harsh breath. But she could not allow herself to understand, or believe, until he seized her.

Then it was too late for thought. The body believed what the mind could not, and the body responded to powerful aggression with powerful defense. Astonishing strength waited in Hannah's thin body. She kicked, and missed; but caught him in the stomach. He grabbed her foot, jerked her over, and fell on her. His weight held her squashed while he fumbled at the neck of her dress. To tear the cloth he had to raise himself a little. Hannah's fighting body breathed air, felt a handbreadth of space, and jerked violently sideways. The dress ripped. With the ripping sound came a startled gasp from Lott, then a shocking curse. Rolling to her feet, Hannah saw him on his knees, clasping his left shoulder.

She bounded over the stone wall and into the long, hillside grass. Uphill she floundered, stumbling on her torn dress; and paused. Between herself and Lott was darkness. Down to the right a small light flickered: Delight's betty lamp in the kitchen.

Cursing horribly, Lott lurched about in the dark. Hannah heard a twig snap, and one stone roll upon another. His next oath sounded nearer. Fleeing, Hannah caught up her dress in both hands, and dropped what she had been unconsciously holding.

She ran silently, trying not to breathe, down toward the little yellow light.

When she burst in, Delight was bringing the betty lamp from hearth to table. "Glory!" she cried. "Is there a catamount in the garden?"

"Lott." In the flickering light Hannah glanced down at herself, flushed, and grabbed the torn dress together. "Bar the door!"

Clucking, Delight obeyed. "But he won't come in here, he knows *I'm* here."

"Where's Harry?"

"Him? Oh he's over the hill hours gone! Don't fret, now. Friend Flower won't tangle with me." With much patting and soothing chatter, Delight bathed Hannah's back and arms. "I'll mend that in the morning, your papa'll never guess. Men don't notice much, you know. Even if he saw it like it is, he mightn't guess!"

Slowly Hannah's mind realized what had happened. Her first instinct was to scream, "Papa!" to run all the way to Northampton and tell him right now; to be confronted, protected, and rid of Lott.

But then, thinking about it, she began to blush and tremble. Now she wanted to hide the whole ugly matter, cover it up, bury it as in deep earth. She could not bear to have Joel, or anyone, think of her in this connection.

"You know, sweet," Delight chattered softly, "what would happen did this get around. 'Twould not be good for Friend Flower, that's for sure! Nothing so fearsome as a townful of angry Christians! He'd rather deal with wild Indians! But then afterward, you know; then they'd begin to wonder about *you*. They'd talk about you and Flower, and you and young Cook, and maybe even you and Harry Bennett! Pull the sleeve down, sweet, it's all dirty here. So you see, 'tis best if we keep this little matter amongst us, just the three of us. You and me and Flower, yonder. For it is a little matter, you know, nothing to think about ever again. Oh no, he won't try it again! Right this minute he's worryin', worryin', are we goin' to tell. Now, we won't tell; but see, we won't tell Flower we won't tell. See?

"Leave the betty on the hearth. I'll take up the candle. Oh yes, I'm comin to bed with you tonight, be sure of it. Sweet, you're shakin'. Would you like a mug of warm milk? The door's well bolted, yes."

4

Hannah glimpsed Lott, and looked quickly down at her toes. Shame rushed over her. "But no," she realized. "'Tis *he* who should be ashamed!" And she made herself lift her head and look him in the face.

He cringed. He was watching her from around Ginger's smooth rump. "Ayah, he's afraid! He thinks I might tell — and maybe I should!" Certainly she should, but she could not. She could never say the necessary words or watch comprehension dawn on Joel's face. She stared at Lott until he blinked and turned away. He pressed his right hand to his left shoulder; and Hannah noticed, on his sleeve, a pale bloodstain he had tried to wash out.

Ginger shifted and pawed, eager to be unloaded and turned out to pasture. "Whoa!" Joel let loose his good-natured roar, and Cousin Jenny, riding pillion, laughed, swayed, and held onto his waist. She wore a fresh calico, a starched bonnet. As always with Jenny, Hannah felt dowdified. But that did not matter now.

"Papa!" she cried eagerly, and held out her hand.

"What? What is it, Hanny? Whoooa! Hold him,

Flower, you asleep there?" Lott came to Ginger's head, quieting him with a word.

"Did I . . . Didn't I get a letter, Papa?"

"Letter! Who would *you* get a letter from? Cousin Isaak got one, and I exchanged it for his daughter. Jenny's staying the night."

Laughter; shifting and blowing from Ginger; Hannah had to step back, as pebbles and sand flew from under the restless hoofs. Her outstretched hand sank to her side.

"Get yourself down, Jenny," Joel spluttered. "Go find a bit of housework to do before I set you to weed onions!"

Jenny patted his shoulder lightly, familiarly, and slid down Ginger's rounded side. She came tripping to Hannah, smiling past Hannah to Harry, in the open door. "Aren't you pleased?" She whispered to Hannah, tossing back a stray ringlet.

"Pleased as Punch," Hannah assured her mournfully. Her world was dim. Pretty Jenny, restless Ginger, and the afternoon sunshine faded, dreamlike, behind the vision of the letter she should have received. The yearning rose in her heart like a song to its climax, and slowly faded.

"That's who I been waitin' to see," Delight cackled, "Jenny Stone! I got a piece of work waitin' for you ain't nobody else can do!"

The "piece of work" Delight had in mind was berry picking. Within minutes she had sent the three young people striding up the pasture. Harry and Jenny trotted ahead, skipping among mica-sparkled rocks, jumping low junipers, jingling their milk buckets together. Hannah trudged in the rear.

As little girls, Hannah and Jenny had often climbed these fields. Bonneted and pinafored, buckets strung from their necks, they had passed whole days in the shade of a high bush. They would pick now and then, eating half of what they picked, and chat. They would watch a hawk circle lazily in the wide sky, and listen to the twittering talk of phoebe and wren. Near the top, where the woods began, they sometimes encountered wild creatures. Once a porcupine bristled at them from a low hemlock branch. Once a mother skunk quietly crossed their path, leading three wobbling infants. Another time a small deer leaped up from behind a juniper and soared away, his white tail floating above him like a thistledown flag.

Hannah had not berried here since she had put up her hair. Memories waited by every rock and bush. Perhaps Delight had hoped to send Hannah back to a peaceful childhood hour; to dilute the ugly memory of last night, wash her mind again in innocence. But the shock was too strong, and her disappointment too profound, to yield to memories. Half paralyzed by misery, she dawdled well behind the happy couple, whose laughter drifted back down the sun-drenched slope.

"And *that* was what the old witch had planned!" Jenny whispered in bed that night.

Hannah retorted sharply, "Don't you call Delight an old witch!"

"Oh, I don't mean it. She's always been my idea of a witch, that's all." Jenny snuggled down between the stiff, homespun sheets, drawing her nightdress tight about her ankles. This, too, recalled childhood; this cozy whispering in the dark, closed in together behind drawn curtains, touched with moonlight. Jenny felt warmly soft. "How did you ever get hold of her?" she was asking. "Is she a relation of yours? Papa said once that Cousin Joel bought her; but that can't be. You can't *buy* a white woman."

"Well, yes, you can. In a way."

"How do you mean?" Jenny rose on her elbow. Her braid, looped across the pillow, smelled of lilac.

"Papa bought her at town meeting. He needed someone at home to manage things. The town was selling her off, you know, to whoever would pay her keep. They didn't *call* it a sale, of course, but that's what it was. Cousin Isaak bid for her, too."

"Goodness." Jenny shook her head, and the braid whispered on the pillow. "Gracious. She had no family at all?"

"I never heard of any. She had a husband, but he died."

"Ayah." Jenny sighed. "One can't manage alone, can one. For so many things, one needs a man." She paused, and added, "I used to worry. You know?"

"About . . . men?"

"Would I get one."

Hannah laughed, shortly, but gently. "You always knew you would."

"No, I didn't. I used to lie awake, making up schemes. Even now . . ."

Roused to mild curiosity, Hannah probed. "Even now?"

"Even now it's far from sure."

"I saw you behind the chokecherries! It looked quite sure to me."

Jenny giggled. Her feet wriggled happily. *"That* part's sure! But you see, it's money. Money or land we must have, or Papa won't hear of it." Impulsive Jenny caught Hannah's thin hand to her breast. "How I envy you, Hanny!"

"What for can you envy me?"

"Why! Even when we were little, I envied you for not having brothers to pull your hair!"

"But I wanted brothers. I used to pray to God to give me one." She had never said that before. Perhaps it had been her prayer that had killed Emma.

"Oh. I suppose our house seems cozy and merry to you — and sometimes it is. But there come times when you need to be alone. There were times I'd have given my new hair ribbon to be alone with Mother, like you. And now, now I'm thinking about what's going to happen, and all, well, now I envy you even more, having all this inheritance to yourself. Nobody to divide with."

Hannah was shocked. "Jennifer Stone! What *do* you mean! I never even thought about that! I'd die of shame!" She jerked upright, stiff with horror. It was not quite true that she had never thought about it. But she had never let herself go on thinking about it; because to think of herself "owning" the house and fields was to think of Joel, dead.

"Oh, lie down! I know what you mean. But one does have to think about the future, what's going to happen. You have a future, Hanny, it's all taken care of. That's why I envy you. Don't look so shocked, you asked!" Softly, Jenny patted the pillow till Hannah sank back down in bed. "There, that's better. I suppose you think that's uncertain, too, because Cousin Joel doesn't like Caleb."

Hannah jerked. "You know?"

"Well surely, the whole town knows. But you see, if Caleb comes home to stay, your papa will like him fine. Cousin Joel's a very lonely man, Hanny. He can't bear for you to go out to Ohio and leave him. And you can't really blame him for that."

Hannah turned that over in her mind. "You say Papa is *lonely?*"

"The loneliest man in the world, that's what my papa says. Does Caleb write you letters?"

"He promised he would. But he hasn't yet. I thought for sure I'd have a letter yesterday."

Jenny patted Hannah's shoulder. "Take heart. Next week Papa's going to Northampton. Maybe you'll get one then."

They whispered a while longer, softer, with longer and longer pauses. Hannah knew she was falling asleep when she saw Lott cringing, holding onto his bloodstained shoulder. She longed to unburden her heart to Jenny, but Jenny would surely tell her sisters, who would tell their friends. And someday one would say to her, "But surely, the whole town knows!" And her flesh crawled at the thought of even Jenny knowing.

Sinking farther into sleep, she knew why Lott held his shoulder. "It was the bayonet. I forgot I held it." She saw it fall from her hands, into long grass.

Next morning Hannah went quietly out by the garden and up the hill, and searched in the grass. She searched several mornings. But Noah Stone's bayonet was lost for good and all.

5

Under dripping lilacs Hannah waited. Welcome rain blew in her face and puddled the path about her feet. She tugged her wool shawl tight about her shoulders and blinked into the rain, watching the bend in the path.

Any minute now Cousin Isaak would be rounding that bend, bringing the Post.

Behind her the house stood silent. Delight and Mouser were doubtless snug on the hearth together. Lott was probably asleep in the shed. A chickadee chirped in the lilacs, then fell silent. The swish of rain and rush of wind in the maples mingled in Hannah's ears with purely imaginary hoofbeats.

She had almost given up, was in fact turning back to the house, when she caught the true sounds of a real approach; a clop of shod hooves, a creak of leather and a roll of stones. She whirled, clutched the shawl to her chest, and darted toward the bend.

But it was not Cousin Isaak who hove into view, wiry and cheerful on his well-preserved nag; the horse was Ginger, shaking his head and blowing from the long climb. Joel bounced about on his back like a fat boy riding a calf. He drew rein beside Hannah.

"If you're waiting for a letter, it ain't here." He patted his pocket.

Hannah's heart chilled. "You have the Post, Papa?"

"Met Isaak at the mill."

"You're *sure* there's nothing for me?"

Joel's face shifted. The craggy lines softened for a moment. But he repeated, "Nothing here," patting his pocket.

Hannah drooped. The wind fingered sharply through her shawl. Rain froze her face. Slowly she squelched up the bank, into the house. Delight called from the hearth, "Word from the Gent?" When Hannah hung up her shawl without answering, she lapsed into unwonted silence. The spinning wheel whirred comfortably. Wrapped around her foot, Mouser purred. The fire snapped and murmured, glowing in its black cavern. Hannah drew the small settle before the hearth, and sank onto it. Through the window she saw Joel pass, saddle on shoulder, heading for the shed. A little later he came back toward the door. He walked slowly, stooped. Delight glanced out, saw him, and stopped her wheel. Muttering to herself she rose abruptly, and skittered out to the buttery, almost closing the door on Mouser's tail. The house was drowned in the sound of water, spring water and rain together.

Heavily, Joel came in. He hung up his coat and

pulled a chair before the fire. Heavily, he let himself down.

Hannah glanced sideways at him. Out in the rain Lott whistled to the horses. In the buttery Delight began a soft hymn. For the first time that Hannah could remember, father and daughter sat together, idle, by the morning fire.

When Delight's hymn swelled enough to cover his voice, Joel spoke softly. "Everything I do is for you. All this . . ." — he gestured vaguely around the dark room — "all this will be for you and your husband, for I have no son." He paused, watching her. "Flower's a good fellow. Good worker."

She flared. "Do you know he tried to . . . tried to . . ." She struggled to say the unsayable.

"Ayah."

Hannah froze. Joel smiled sadly. " 'Twon't happen again, I assure you. I've got Flower's word on that. But I was hoping you had learned something, there. I hoped you might notice that Flower's a man. That way, it might do us a bit of good, that nastiness. Was I too far wrong?"

Hannah swallowed collected spittle. "You wanted . . . you want *that much* . . ."

"Ayah." Joel raised his voice to a normal pitch, for Delight was now crooning loudly. "I want for you to wed Lott Flower, who is a strong worker. And I want for us to live together in this warm, tight house that I built up for you. And I want to trot grandbabies on my knee at this hearth. And now, Hannah; what is it *you* want?"

Hannah hid her face in her damp hands. What is it I want? Nobody ever asked me that before. Did I ask it myself? Or have I been wandering in dreams, thoughtless, as a ewe wanders in a stony pasture?

The fire hissed. In the buttery, Delight screeched:

Oh cease my wandering soul
On restless wing to roam.

All this wide world from pole to pole
Has not for thee a home!

Through her fingers, Hannah said. "I want to go away."

Joel laughed, miserably. "I build the girl a house, and she wants to go away."

"Ayah. I want to build my own house."

Silence followed this. After a while Joel said hopefully, "Maybe young Cook has got himself married by now. They do things fast in Ohio." Hannah squeezed her fingers against her eyes. In another while, Joel said, "You go build your own house, you leave me by myself here. You thought about that?" Hannah nodded. Confused tears wet her fingers. From the buttery echoed a triumph shout:

Behold the ark of God!
Behold the open door!
Oh haste to gain that dear abode,
And rove, my soul, no more!

6

Bells rang over the hillside. Balancing on the stile, hugging a jug of cold switchel, Hannah looked upfield.

A long line of men, an army of neighbors, stood sharpening scythes. Lott was closest to Hannah. Beyond him stood Harry Bennett, and Joel, and Cousin Isaak, and his four sons, and several Cooks. Each held his upended scythe in one hand, in the other his whetstone; and as stone struck steel, bell-like music rang across the mowing.

Lott was bare to the waist. His arms and chest were hairy-black. The sinews of his arms were like hemp cords, wound around. Hannah came slowly up toward him, repelled, yet fascinated. "Nothing can happen here," she thought, "Of course, nothing can happen now." Still, she approached him as a robin might approach a sleeping cat.

Lott tipped black hair from his eyes, slipped the whetstone into his pocket, and saw Hannah. He grinned, and flicked his left shoulder with a quick finger. The scar was healing. "Leave the jug under the first maple," he said, as she passed behind him. The next moment he drew back the scythe, stepped forward and swung. The whole line of men swung together, the army advanced across the mowing; whispering grasses fell.

Hannah climbed slowly, lugging the heavy jug. The switchel — spring water and vinegar — was cold against her stomach; sunshine was hot on her shoulders.

A sharp whistle sounded above. Hannah rested, balancing the jug on her hip, and saw a jaunty figure skipping down the field path.

Jenny bounded happily along, swinging her skirts in one hand, in the other a scrap of paper. "For you!" She cried, waving the paper. "Post from Northampton!"

Hannah waited, not expectantly. She did not recognize her answered prayer because the messenger and the manner were not what she expected. "I hid it in my shirtwaist," Jenny panted, closer. "Cousin Joel won't like it!" She bounded down the last hillock and held the paper out to Hannah, Hannah set down the jug and looked.

The paper was tight-folded and sealed; unevenly addressed to "Hannah Stone, Spinster, Winterfield, Northampton, Massachusetts, Paid." Hannah looked; stared; cried out and snatched. The paper trembled in her hands and tore with the seal.

"My dear Hannah," she read slowly. "Why have You not replid to my leters? Have y changed Yr Mind about our agreement? I have not changed my Mind and wil not til I hear from Y. If We stil agree I will go for Y in the spring. I told Y prospects here so will not repeat. Yr faithful Friend — "

" 'Why have you not replied to my letters!' " Hannah cried, "Letters! More than one! Oh Jenny, what has happened!"

Jenny's comforting arms went round her. "Letters are lost," she consoled, "and he is so far away. Only think, Hanny, a little scrap of paper, to travel so far!"

But Hannah trembled with grief, thinking of Caleb watching, hoping for the Post, even as she had done. "He thinks I have changed my mind! He thinks, the Lord knows what!"

"Well now, you must answer him. Here is the address."

"Answer him! Oh Lord, how do I answer him?"

"Tell him you haven't changed your mind. Do you have paper, Hanny?"

Hannah tried to collect herself. Paper. Did they have paper in the house? "Well, no."

"I'll get you paper."

"Bless you!"

"Next time someone goes to Northampton."

"Oh." It was a rare neighbor who would take time now, in haying season, for a trip to town.

"Don't look so forlorn, dear! We'll have paper in a week or so. Meantime, you can make ink."

"Letters." Hannah mourned, looking the missive over. "He has sent me letters. Perhaps all summer he has been writing, and had no answer!"

"Hide it," Jenny warned abruptly. "They're coming back."

Hannah moaned, "How could they all be lost!"

Jenny snatched the letter and thrust it down her dress. "Dry your eyes!"

Hannah blinked back rising tears. Tall before her, the grass was a nodding blur of green and gold. A scythe flashed, the green blur toppled; and Joel grinned triumph, dark above the fallen brightness.

7

Two days after, they teddered the hay. Hannah and Lott worked the slope above the house. Across the stone wall Joel and Delight worked the larger mowing; Harry had gone to mow the Bennett field that day.

They had worked since the dew was dry, and now the sun was at its zenith. Hannah's arms and shoulders ached. Her eyes ached if she tried to look away beyond the bonnet-shade. Her dress stuck and clung everywhere about her. Exhausted, she drove her pitchfork into the next grass heap and let it stand while she straightened her sore back, shaded her eyes, and gazed about the field.

The stone wall swam sickly in heat waves. But there in the corner, shade washed over the stones — cool shade, leaf-whispering. The switchel jug was stashed among those rocks. Very slowly, Hannah moved into the shade.

She sank upon a stone and leaned against another. Shade enveloped her, as water would, could one swim.

"They'll get ahead of us, the oldsters!"

The shadow blocking the flow of coolness was Lott. He stood before her, pitchfork in hand, grinning through sweat. Sweat stood out on his neck, his forehead, his hands. Hannah drew away, as far as the rock at her back would let her.

"Your pa and the old biddy, you think they've stopped in the shade? They'll have the laugh on us!"

"I don't care," Hannah murmured.

Lott laughed. "I don't care neither, I tell you why. They've got nothing to talk about, see. Now us, we've got talking to do." He jammed his pitchfork to stand, and dropped down beside Hannah. "No, don't fret" — for she was straining away— "I'm no more keen on sport right now than you! But here's a chance to talk, and no one listening. Look, Hannah. I like you."

Hannah looked into Lott's face, closer to her than ever before in daylight. It was not an ugly face; homely, yes. The small, black eyes fixed on hers were not mean, as she had thought, only alien. And Lott was trying to be friendly.

"To be honest, I like the farm." He waved a hand downhill. "Snug house, spring water, tight shed. Wouldn't anyone not like it! But here's the thing. Your papa likes me. He's got it planned, see. You and me, we marry. No, wait! Hear me out. He gets to have family around him, then he leaves us the farm. He's going to be around a long time yet, I wouldn't bet on him taking to his bed for a while; but him and me, we work together like a matched pair, you know that. So there you are. He gets family, we get the farm. What do you think?"

Hannah was silent. The stench of the man took her breath. The future he outlined numbed her mind.

Lott watched her. The earnest, plausible young man who had peered momentarily out of his eyes retreated, and the mocking swaggerer returned. "I know what you're thinking. You're thinking. 'My, but this Lott Flower's a homely fellow, next to my Caleb!' Ain't you!"

Hannah shrank small as Lott's face darkened. He stood up and grasped the standing pitchfork. God be thanked, Hannah thought, he's going. She made a small gesture of going, herself, pushing a foot forward, preparing to stand.

But Lott talked on, rumbling like a gathering storm. "Hannah Stone, you are the biggest fool in Winterfield! You think your Caleb's going to come riding back some morning, and pull you up on a pillion, and ride you off to the plains of gold? I tell you, your Caleb is dead in some tavern!" Hannah made a small sound. "Or if he ain't dead, he's wed, and that's the same thing to you! And if he ain't wed" — Lott yanked the pitchfork out of the ground — "if he ain't wed he's bedded with some whore! But he ain't bought no farm, nor he ain't never coming back to Winterfield, never!" As he cried *never,* Lott emphatically drove the pitchfork forward and down.

Hannah's gaze was riveted to his furious face. She watched it crumple from fury to horror. He gaped, and moaned.

Then she looked down. The pitchfork stood, quivering. Two of its iron tines were embedded in earth. The third was embedded in her shoe.

While Hannah stared, Lott yanked the fork out. The tine left a deep, round hole. Blood welled from that hole like water from the spring. Red and thick and slimy, it gushed over the dirty black shoe.

Lott flung himself down and tore at the shoe. Rough with desperation, he rushed the shoe off the foot. The hole went deep into the foot, between the first and second toes. Blood welled steadily. Looking at it, Hannah began to feel jagged pain.

High and frantic, a scream sounded near, and echoed. Hannah did not recognize the voice as her own.

In the next field the old people paused, pitchforks raised, listening. At the next scream they dropped the forks and ran for the stone wall, Joel's boots thudding like heavy hoofs, Delight's patched skirts flying.

8

A small summer fire drowsed on the hearth. At hot midmorning the door stood wide, inviting sunshine and flies. Flies droned, undisturbed, around the vegetables, in the milk, and inside Hannah's head.

She leaned over the round plank table, cutting squash and beans for the noon dinner. Half kneeling on a chair, she rested her paining foot. The wound sucked and quivered, and the muscles near it seemed to jump and start like fleas. A week ago a scab had formed over the wound itself. But then the whole foot puffed and turned blue. Red lines speared jaggedly up the ankle. Delight dunked the foot in icy spring water over Hannah's protests. She brought clean, new homespun to wrap it; though when she tore the good cloth, Hannah wept. Not for this had she spun and woven! Delight set her lips tight, ripped the new cloth, and bound up the foot with tallow.

Delight was carrying more than twice her usual work load. Besides doing most of Hannah's work she helped Joel and Harry in the field. Lott had disappeared. When Joel carried Hannah down the hill he

paused at the spring to wash the new wound, and
roared to Lott to help. No Lott came running. Lott
was nowhere to be seen. "If he knows what's good
for him," Joel growled, "he'll never poke his nose
around this door again!" Apparently, Lott knew what
was good for him.

It was no good, being an invalid. Daily Hannah
struggled with pain and guilt. Each morning she
climbed determinedly out of bed — "Today I'll be
well" — only to crumple and cry as her foot touched
the floor. Having once managed the steep stairs down
to the kitchen, she remained there. Even the trip to
the backhouse was too much, halfway there, her foot
would begin to throb "fit to kill!" That meant chamber
pots, more work for Delight. Hannah insisted on doing
the cooking. "I cook with my hands, not my foot. And
I'm in here, anyway." And so she dragged and hopped
about the kitchen, needing half a day to prepare a
simple meal.

This morning even cutting squash was exhausting
work. Leaning over made her head ache ferociously;
and the back of her neck throbbed. "It's hurt for two
days," she thought, "or is it three? Here comes Delight
— Lord, make her stop humming!" Delight's croon,
approaching down the stairs, was suddenly more than
Hannah could bear. Lest she should cry out, "Oh be
quiet, do!" she crammed a chunk of squash into her
mouth. Her jaws clamped on it, independent of her
will, as though they would never let go.

A fly buzzed loudly in the butter bowl. Hannah laid
down her knife and held her buzzing head in both
hands. Delight's soft, moccasined thumping down the
stairs banged in her head. "Mr. Bennett," Delight
squealed, "did you bring the Post?" Hannah wrenched
her head around on her stiff, aching neck. She squinted
toward the light.

Harry and Jenny stood together on the doorstone.
They laughed and swayed, a moving patchwork of too-
bright color. Hannah closed her eyes. She heard Jen-

ny's quick steps. The floor trembled under Harry's tread, and Hannah trembled with it. She forced her jaws open, poked out the squash with her finger, and said, "Post?" In the answering silence, she slitted her eyes to look up.

Jenny stood by, looking anxious. Slowly she untied her bonnet and took it off. "I think I'll stay with you, Hanny. You look unwell."

"Unwell!" Harry remarked from the other side. "She looks — "

"Tch-tch-tch!" Delight came running. The scuffle of her moccasins set Hannah's teeth on edge. "Sweet, maybe you'd like to go to bed for a while."

Hannah tried to say "Post" again, but the effort was too much. Instead she pushed a begging hand, palm up, toward Harry's voice. Delight understood. "She wants to see the Post first. Then she'll come to bed like a lamb."

Harry's voice said, "What on earth for — Oh. Yes." A rustle of papers — in Hannah's head a rumble of stones — and the letters were rattled out, splayed across the table. Hannah leaned to examine the names. They were roughly, unevenly written, some she could not make out at all. "Little," she read, "Fiske, Reverend, no Stone." Her forehead sank upon the table, and rested.

"Delight!" Jenny's voice echoed in a cavern in Hannah's brain. "She is truly ill!"

"Come, I'll carry her. Run ahead, Jen, open the doors." Harry's arms were under Hannah and around her, and lifting. For the second time she found herself being raised and carried like a little child. Squinting over Harry's leather shoulder she saw the kitchen recede: fireplace, table, blurred white wall and candlestand. Passing the open door she glimpsed a hurtful golden brightness. On the steep stairs Harry began to puff; she felt his breath shaking her body, which, when he laid it on the bed behind the white curtain, con-

tinued to tremble and twitch and shudder with alien
breath.

There in the decent, curtained dimness, pain grew
into terror. Hannah felt every sound in the house. If a
helpful neighbor breathed in the hall, Hannah
twitched. If a pot clanged on the hearth downstairs,
her back arched, and her limbs went off entirely on
their own. It was often necessary for Delight to change
the sheets, for Hannah could not in any way manage
a chamber pot; and in her crawling, jerking agony, she
forgot to be ashamed. Meanwhile, her throat closed.

Once Joel's face hung over her, dark and heavy. She
was awake, watching, and she saw his face change.
The hairy nostrils flared, the eyes widened and glazed.
Like a child, Joel pressed a fist to his mouth and drew
back, letting the curtain fall.

In her father's fright Hannah read horror. And now
her own terror congealed into horror, and she knew.
"This thing is the end of me." Knowing that she would
never again rise from the bed and dowse her face in
the basin on the commode, she was almost too weary
to care. "If I could only sleep, I'd gladly sleep forever." Only the thought of dowsing her face stirred
longing.

A strange face once thrust into her darkness; a man
peering, muttering in his beard, fumbling in a bag for
spectacles so that he could peer closer. He withdrew,
the curtain dropped behind him. "No matter," he said
loudly, "even had you sent sooner" — and Hannah
convulsed violently.

Delight sometimes moistened a cloth and patted
cold water over Hannah's face and body. Dumbly,
impatiently, she awaited this kindness. A drop of water might slip between her stiff lips, and even down
her throat.

Buried now in throbbing heat, she dreamed of the
spring. She followed the trough to the buttery, and
stooped beside the bucket, and drank from her cupped
hands.

There came a moment when a triangle of faces hung above her. Joel was closest; above him Jenny, and at her right shoulder, Delight. She saw them as in the wavering light of a single candle, a light so mild it hardly hurt her eyes. From beyond sounded murmurs and shufflings, and a door closing. But Hannah's muscles did not react. No spasm threatened, unless it was the tightening in her chest.

From waist to parched mouth she was an iron rod. Air passed achingly down the rod and up again, in and out. She wished that Joel would reach out his big hands and rip the rod open and let the air definitely in, or out.

The light wavered, and failed. Hannah looked into a cave of darkness. It was cool in the cave, it was restfully cold, and Hannah yearned toward it. Then a radiance burst, like a seedpod of light.

Brighter than life, more intensely seen, a little girl clasped a puppy in scrawny arms. She was a thin child, neatly dressed in drab homespun, with black braids looped over her ears. She held the puppy toward her papa — Joel. He shook his head. When she persisted he stepped close and gave both child and pup a sharp cuff. As he turned away, Hannah saw his desolate eyes. "Poor Papa!" she thought, although it was the child who cried.

The scene sank into darkness, and another light-pod burst in its place. Candles beamed on the round plank table. Ruddy in candlelight, Joel reached for the posset pot. He was laughing, telling a story to plump Emma. She leaned her knitting toward the light and laughed with him. Little Black-Braids was laughing too, not because of the story, which she did not follow, but because she was happy. She kept one small hand on her mother's knee, and tilted back her head to watch her father over the table. Her pointed chin reached just above the table. Hannah knew how the maternal knee felt to the child's hand — firm and warm. The little girl felt encased in love, as in a bright, warm quilt. But the quilt melted away. The firm knee dissolved in air; the child's hand groped, empty.

Flashed a summer scene: taller, now, Hannah stood on the bank above the lilac bushes. She watched with awe as shouting, vigorous neighbors swarmed up and down ladders, and hammers echoed from the roof. Joel, in command, stood astride the new ridgepole. Down on the grass, neighbors' wives were spreading dinner on trestle tables. They looked up, and admired; but Goodwife Cook flapped her apron and shouted at her little Caleb, who was running along the ridgepole.

He ran to the chimney and touched it, as he had been dared to do. Twisting his bright head, looking gleefully down, he caught Hannah's wide eye, and stuck out his tongue.

All this time Hannah had been drawing closer to the cold mouth of the dark cave, and now she was almost inside it. Cold, peaceful darkness closed around her. Pain dimmed and fell away, the relief was heaven itself. But one last scene burst upon the blackness in color brighter than sunlight. Directly before her she saw Caleb's profile. He was thirteen; freckles dusted his nose. His red curls were crushed under a brown woolen cap; and just beyond him a brown mass moved, a white patch gleamed. An ox's eye, golden and kind, looked over Caleb's shoulder.

Now tiny, rapid scenes twirled together like dancers. Joel sat smoking at the hearth, his gouty feet pillowed on a hassock; Delight pounded bread dough on the table; Caleb swung onto the brown mare's back, and away; and Hannah saw herself, invisible, among the lilacs.

She called to Caleb, but no voice escaped. A jagged, piercing breath, the last of pain, dragged in and wheezed out. Hannah drifted up, away from the bed.

Drifting free and painless, she looked down on Joel and Delight and Jenny. They seemed insubstantial, shadowy. She looked through their clumsy garments at warm skin, and through warm skin, to amazing pumpings and flowings, fiery tides of life. Life-fire crackled around their phantom outlines, like pale lightning.

Jenny knelt down by the bed and buried her face in her hands. Delight rocked back on her heels. Tears squeezed slowly from her wrinkled, tight-shut eyes. Joel was stepping slowly, jerkily backward; away. Hannah was behind him, yet she could see his face. "Poor Papa!"

And now the world was shadowy, the house a dimness, haunted by dream-figures. Summer sunshine beat at the windows, white light, like the light seen in dreams. Somewhere beyond this shone true light.

Still dreaming, a sleeper comes half awake, feeling sunlight warm on closed eyes. So Hannah felt the touch of deep light. "Who am I?" She asked herself, as a dreamer does. "Where am I?" The knowledge was beyond her, she was still more than half asleep; but she felt herself happy, the coming morning one of joy. She felt as she had felt when she was little, and woke on a rare, holiday morning; conscious that no work or school waited, that there was to be instead an excursion, sunshine, delight; though why, or what that delight, she was still too dream-fogged to remember.

Like a waking dreamer Hannah strove to open her eyes. But something held her back. "The dream is not quite finished." And she saw Caleb leaning from his saddle. "Have you changed your mind?"

Deliberately, Hannah closed her eyes against the insisting light. She turned over and went back to sleep, sinking again into dream. But she could not sink all the way, the dream would not take on light and color. Weightless, she drifted through the dark, insubstantial house. About her the house dissolved in gray mist. No need to float down the stairs, foggy walls opened before her, she sank through timbers and ceiling into the kitchen, where gathered shadows were phantom neighbors. Goodwife Bennett, a lumpy mist, dark-burning, stood at the table. Nancy and Eunice worked on the hearth. Reverend Jones flamed by the door.

Out across the doorstone Hannah floated, into the white imaginary light. Down the bank she glided, in among the lilacs. She was now nearly deep asleep; but still conscious of the brightness pressing on her eyelids. Morning waited, and joy. "Only a little longer," Hannah told herself, "only a little more sleep."

The lilacs slept more deeply than Hannah, more deeply even than the phantoms haunting the shadow-house. Unconsciously, the lilacs stretched and reached toward the sun. At intervals they dropped brown, stiff leaves; or, swimming up through sleep almost into dream they opened new leaves, and fragrant, heavy flowers.

The Nest 1850

Which of your children do you love the most?
The one who is sick, until he is well.
The one who is absent, until he returns.

—*Anonymous*

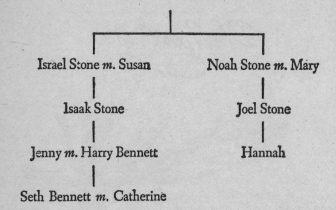

Israel Stone *m.* Susan   Noah Stone *m.* Mary

Isaak Stone   Joel Stone

Jenny *m.* Harry Bennett   Hannah

Seth Bennett *m.* Catherine

1

The children were playing in the blue snowfield. Full March moonlight flooded the snow. From the high sugarhouse clear down to the road, the crust shone glassy. Intersecting ridges were actually buried stone walls, lined with naked maples whose blue shadows laced the field.

The sleds zipped across the shadows, flashed over the walls, gleamed in high flight; then crashed to crust and sliced down toward the road, trailing happy shrieks. Uphill stomped small, stubborn figures, dragging dead weights of sleds, barrel staves or ripper sleds. The climb took long enough for the moon to shift, tilting the maple shadows at slightly new angles. The swooping, flying descent took only moments, just long enough for Catherine Bennett to stand up from the crowded table in the sugarhouse and waddle outside to the moonlight. She drew her shawl close as she came out, for the air was sharp; and out here, no one would notice.

Within her the child rolled and squirmed and swam. She called him Orin. When he had kicked, back there

in the sugarhouse, she had glanced down and seen
her gray woolen dress actually bump the table. She
looked hastily about, searching the faces around her
for suppressed mirth, or shock. Only Letty appeared
to notice. She stared pointedly for a long moment
while her spoon dripped syrup. Then, recalling herself,
she popped the maplewax daintily into her prim
mouth. But Catherine pushed herself up, smiling ex-
cuses, and barreled outside just in time to see the
Fiske boy's ripper careen onto the icy road a quarter-
mile below. She plainly heard the crunch and whine
of crust; for the frozen air echoed like a bell.

It was not Catherine's fault that she was here in
company, instead of moping about the house alone.
She had not wanted to come; rather, she had not let
herself want to come. "It's too near time," she told
her husband, Seth; and blushed. This was the first
mention ever made of Orin.

Seth guffawed. "I reckon they've all seen a woman
in the family way before! If the youngsters notice,
tell 'em you et too much sugarsnow and maybe they'll
quit gobbling! You don't want to sit home and knit
while the biddies gossip, now do you?"

Catherine had not so much as gone to church since
Orin showed. But she could have wept at the thought
of the biddies gossiping without her. She wrapped
a loose shawl around her pear shape and stood square
against the glow from the firebox, never sideways.
No one said a word about her shape except old Mrs.
Cook, who remarked, as she always did, that Catherine
was getting even fatter; and the new doctor in town
gave her a conspiratorial smile. The children, whose
sharp eyes she had feared, were much too busy pack-
ing and hustling pans — and gobbling — to pay her
any mind. Satisfied at last, they surged outdoors in an
eager tide; and the crunch of crust and wind-choked
shrieks punctured the adult merriment indoors.

Catherine sat near the middle of the long table,
across from Letty. Happily, she listened to old Mrs.

Cook's recipe for Indian pudding; told Amy Partridge about cornstarch for diaper rash; and listened to Seth trying out his wit on new Dr. Peters.

"February twelve," Seth was saying loudly, "I went out of chore and found all my Merinos frozen stiff, lying about like logs with their feet in the air.". .

Bewildered, Dr. Peters shook his learned had. "I never suspected sheep could freeze to death! Farming is certainly a risky business."

Seth gave him a sharp look and ducked his head.

Catherine leaned forward. "Dr. Peters, why did you move out here? I mean . . ." She blushed. Her round face tingled from dimpled chin to sunny, upswept hair. She had meant no rudeness, she only wanted to divert the innocent stranger from the question of sheep, and Seth's ill-concealed mirth. "I mean, there must be ever so many more sick people in Northampton . . ." Dr. Peters gave her his attention. It was then that he smiled in that knowing way, making her blush even pinker.

"Mama." A slight tap on the shoulder. Catherine reached a warm arm around Nellie's plump waist and pulled her close. A small shake of her head warned, "Don't interrupt, dear. Grownups are talking." Nellie leaned against her, the unvoiced complaint beating in her sturdy little body like a pulse.

At some length, Dr. Peters explained that his wife needed country air. Therefore, he had bought the Squire Winter farm, the highest, most isolated house in Winterfield. "As the crow flies, it's five miles due north of here. By carriage road you turn at the sawmill . . ."

Catherine hugged Nellie and smiled pleasantly across at Dr. Peters, nodding whenever he paused. She was not listening. Indeed, she had little more patience for this discourse than had the child. Her little ones were usually healthy. Seth's vitality was legendary in town; and for herself, when her time came she would be calling Mrs. Pease, the midwife, who sat just down the table, chatting patiently with Mrs. Cook. At last Dr. Peters paused longer than usual, and Nellie seized the moment. "Mama, Harry won't let us on the ripper. And we helped make it!"

Catherine turned to the little girl in the circle of her arm. Nellie was plump and blue-eyed. Bright ringlets framed her rosy cheeks. She looked like the child-heroine of a story paper. Jane, peering shyly over her shoulder, was dark, skinny, a trifle cross-eyed, just like her mother, Letty. Catherine thought Jane was most likely the one Harry did not want on the ripper. With his eager, robust sister Harry was usually affable. But Jane was supposed to be delicate. Letty was forever saying it, so that Jane herself knew it; and she tended to mince and simper.

"Mama," Nellie urged, "come talk to Harry. Please tell him he's got to take us down, 'cause we helped make it."

Shep came wandering along, pushing his long nose between guests, flailing them with his heavy tail. Slowly he plodded through the sweet steam, hunting for Nellie. Shoving between the girls, he laid his nose in Nellie's hand. Catherine was reminded.

"Nell, aren't you minding Baby?"

"Grandpa's got him. He said for Jane and me to go slide, but Harry won't let us."

Tilting carefully backward, holding onto the table, Catherine looked down the row of backs to the firebox. Under the high stone arch the fire glowed rosy. Harry Bennett, Seth's ancient father, stooped across the red light. Long spoon in hand, he awaited the exactly right moment to pour. This was his specialty, a chore he would delegate to no one while he could stand in his boots. Beside him stooped a little, skirted figure, with curls like flames: Baby Myron.

Sometimes while kneading or scrubbing or peeling — whenever her active mind wandered — Catherine thought about Baby Myron versus Orin. One day soon, Baby would find himself abruptly promoted to

Myron. "That'll put his nose out of joint!" Mrs. Cook would chortle. Did it have to? Could she somehow soften the blow? Now she was glad to see Myron bending over the sap, imitating Grandpa's stance and gesture. Myron was beginning to become a boy. Nine months ago, this might almost have saddened her. Now, she was relieved.

"All right," she said to Nellie. "You go out. I'll come talk to Harry." Just then Orin squirmed inside her, turned over, and kicked the table. Catherine was glad to escape Letty's censorious eye and betake herself outdoors, into the cold moonlight. With a crunch and swoosh Harry's ripper took off. Catherine was just in time to see it depart and Tom Fiske's party come to rest in the road below.

"Too late," she said sympathetically to the sad-faced little girls. "But we brought the skates, you know. They're in the woodshed. Why don't you two go skate? Harry'll be all night coming." She was not joking. The snow-crust shone like ice, clear down to the road. Catherine remembered skating on such crust herself, when she was light and little. It would uphold a small, flying form whose weight lasted only an instant on any one spot.

"Come on, Jane, let's do!" Nellie grabbed Jane's hand. Off to the workshed they ran, Shep bounding after. Catherine thought Jane was probably relieved. She was not adventurous like Nellie. Perhaps she had not really wanted to rip down the long hill at all!

Harry's ripper reared to the top of the first stone wall, and flew over. "HAW!" Harry yelled above the shrieks. "HAW!" Thunderous, the ripper hit crust and flashed across the lower, steeper field, swerving toward the highest projection of the next wall. "GEE-EEE!" Perfectly on target, the ripper soared from the wall, airborne, coats flapping like wings. While Catherine's gravid body stood squarely in the snow, her soul flew with the children, between moonlight and sudden shadow, against the stinging wind.

The ripper crackled down the last slope and whirled about in the road, barely missing the Fiske party, who were just scrambling to their feet. All about them blue snow sparkled. Watching and listening, a little withdrawn, Catherine was flooded by joy, as by moonlight.

Happiness was her usual state. Contentment glowed about her, an almost visible aura, drawing love and confidence from everyone, even against her will. But this commonplace happiness of hers was unconscious, automatic as breath. Now, in a cold, bright moment, brief as Harry's flight from the wall, Catherine was joy-conscious. "I am happy," she knew. And it seemed to her that the sharp air was as joyous as she; the hills were happy. Joy was the sap rising in the great, sleepy maples along the walls. Joy rose from earth to heaven in a constant, yet momentary flame. There were words for it. "All you hills and valleys, bless the Lord," thought Catherine, for the first time with understanding. And she knew that for a moment she had stood at the heart of creation, in the fountain of secret, silent joy that was creation.

"I am alive," she knew. She stretched, arching her strained back, and suddenly felt Death stir within.

Now, that was no way to think! One prepared. One laid away little blankets and shirts and diapers, one hinted to the menfolk to move the sitting-room stove up to the bedroom. One listened to the interior bumps and thumps, and looked for signs of deliverance. But of the actual deliverance, of the hours that would be minutes and the minutes that would be hours, one did not think.

"Never had no trouble before," she said firmly, aloud. "No call to have trouble now." She knew it would be all right. This time next year she would stand again before the sugarhouse. She would smell sweet steam and listen to cheerful voices. And the only difference would be Orin, hanging on her skirt.

"You oughtn't to be here," said a cold voice from the door. "You don't want to take cold *now.*"

"It's brisk," Catherine agreed. "Bites. Almost like a storm coming." The moon mocked the thought.

But Letty said, "Almanac says storm. Come inside, Katie."

"One moment, Lett." Catherine shuddered distaste at that "Katie." It was typical of Letty that she never noticed that reaction. She would still be saying "Katie" when they were toothless old cronies, patchworking together on winter evenings.

Cold though it was, Catherine did not want to leave the scene. She bundled her shawl closer. "Look at the bad boys," she murmured to Letty. Far down in the road, Tom Fiske and Harry were coming to blows. Pale echoes of joy haloed the milling children.

"Jane!" Letty shrilled, "Tighten your scarf!" Hand in hand, two small shadows swooped past, skirts billowing darkly over the creaking crust. Shep ran a short way after them. But when they swept off across the open hilltop he gave up and trotted, panting, back to Catherine.

"Jane was sniffing this morning," Letty lamented. "If she catches her death now — "

"Not while she's having a good time," Catherine assured her. "You never catch your death when you're happy." That was her experience. Letty answered with a snort. The little girls were now fluttering over a distant field. The thin "delicate" figure followed the chunky one, copying every move from a figure eight to an immodest split. "Tch-tch," said Letty. "Katie, do come in!"

Shep waved his tail slowly across Catherine's feet. Cocking his head, he twitched his ears toward the distant groan of crust under skates. Harry and Tom conversed clearly — and fairly peaceably — as they commenced the climb. Their followers argued as to who should drag up the rippers.

"I do believe," said Catherine, "we *are* in for a

storm!" For she knew how sound carries before a storm.

"Naturally," Letty said. "Such a beautiful night — even if it is cold — lovely weather always brings a storm."

2

Two nights later Catherine heard coughing. It woke her from a dream, a bad dream which recurred only when she was in the family way. Toward the end of her pregnancy, when her belly weighed on her heart and breath came short, she would return in dream to an otherwise forgotten moment of childhood: she was standing on the trapdoor in her father's barn. For some reason — perhaps she was playing a game — she jumped up and down. The trapdoor broke and Catherine fell through. It happened so fast she did not realize it was happening until it was over, and she found herself flat on her back, breath knocked out, but miraculously unhurt. But in the dream it happened slowly. Catherine watched the door fall silently away beneath her, into darkness.

In the darkness was terror. A revelation of mortality

waited there, more dreadful than the parson's hell. This sea of anguish underlay ordinary, daily life. There was only a thin trapdoor holding one up. Suddenly, one could fall through.

She was hovering over the open hole of horror when the cough woke her. Gasping relief, she listened. This was the dry, double cough that spells trouble. "Sounds like sage tea and mustard plaster," she thought. But who was it? She wandered drowsily among possibilities, drifting into sleep between names, jerking awake at the next cough.

It was not Seth. His half of their big bed was cold and empty. He and Grandpa were up at the sugarhouse, hard at work; for the sap flowed mightily now, even at night. (Cough!) It was not Baby. His soft, sweet breath came and went, over in the trundle bed. Catherine listened to it with pleasure. Harry's bed was just the other side of the wall. Catherine heard him grinding his teeth through the next "Cough!" It came from Letty's room, across the hall — either Letty herself, or her delicate Jane. Catherine wallowed onto her other side and listened to Orin's gentle, sleepy thumps. Morning would be time enough to deal with the cougher. She sank into sleep.

She woke again when the rooster crowed in the big new barn. The moon was down, the room stiffly cold. For a time she huddled, listening for the cough. None came. Had it cured itself? Unlikely.

She rolled slowly out of bed and bear-danced on the freezing floor while climbing out of her voluminous nightdress and into her daytime wool tent. Kneeling, wriggling and rolling on the bed, she managed to get on her shoes around the squirming bulk of Orin. Now the frost-laced window showed milky white. Catherine could see the bed, and the protruding trundle bed where Baby slept in a nest of quilts. Softly she stepped around it and out into the dark hall, where she paused to crack Harry's door open. "Harry, wake up. I'm going down."

"Uuuuugh," said Harry.

In the dining room Catherine hit warmth. She stood a good minute by the stove, in which a chunk had glowed away all night. The children's clothes were piled on nearby chairs — Harry's vest and shoes, collar and coat; the little girls' and Baby's wool dresses. Catherine opened the stove, poked the embers to life, and added the last chunk from the woodbox. "Harry!" she shouted up the front stairs, "I'm starting up the stove!" Silence answered. Catherine remarked, "Tchtch," Letty-fashion. As soon as the roads were clear and dry, school would recommence; and Harry would have an even harder time getting up in the mornings! "That child sleeps like he had nothing to look forward to." That gave her an idea. "Harry," she yelled up the stairs. "I bet the snow's perfect for snowshoes! Night was freezing!" She was rewarded by a growl.

In the kitchen she started up the drowsing fire in the range and drew the teapot forward onto the heat. Shep came slowly out from behind the range, "smiling," stretching, and waving his foxy brush. Catherine opened the door for him; fetched her shawl and waddled outside. The morning was still, pearly, stinging-cold. "Smells like storm," she told Shep as she set off for the backhouse.

So cold it was, the sap would have slowed, maybe stopped. Sometime this morning the men would be down from the sugarhouse, probably hungry, though they cooked for themselves up there — eggs in bubbling syrup, beans and bacon. Back in the fast-warming kitchen she set spiders and pots of leftovers in the oven; beans, potpie, biscuits, half an apple pie. Giggles and squeals sounded from the dining room.

"Jane." Catherine crossed the little hall and looked into the dining room. "Were you coughing last night?"

Jane hesitated, pulling up a stocking. She sniffed, as though already assaulted by sage tea and mustard plaster. She said, "It stopped by itself."

"Hmph." Catherine went back to the kitchen, to the

mirrorshelf. Now that there was enough white light to
see by, she brushed her long, fair hair and wound it
into a soft bun, munching the while on hairpins. Her
belly pulled her arms down, her back ached. Long
before the bun was smooth she was panting, as though
from a long climb.

Harry barged through, pulling on his cap. His blue
eyes were sleep-laden, he stumbled on a flying shoelace. "Harry," Catherine called through the last hairpins, "it's a sharp morning out there! Button up!"
Mumbling, he went out through the milkroom; and
before he slammed the door, Catherine heard the purl
of water, bubbling in the quiet dark.

This sound distinguished home from all the other
houses Catherine had lived in or visited. Here, you
had only to open the milkroom door to hear the murmur of endless waters, like the voice of God; not the
thunderous Scripture-God, but Catherine's God, the
One Who swelled buds and seeds and Orin. "Gracious!" She laughed at herself. "Fretting about the
Lord, and breakfast not set! I'm losing stiches!" She
patted her bun finally into place and flashed herself a
smile. A pretty woman, almost young, turned from the
mirror to call, "Put places for Papa and Grandpa,
they'll be down." A moment later she went across to
check up.

Nellie was setting the table. At the stove, Letty
struggled to button Baby into his skirt. He twisted and
wriggled and smiled an overjoyed good morning, holding out soft arms to Catherine. Over his curly head
Letty smiled up at her; and Catherine responded to
this woman, whom she almost disliked, with a smile
so radiant it could have been taken for love.

Poor Letty was an object lesson in the folly of
"fretting about the Lord." Josh Bennett, her husband,
was one of Seth's fifty cousins. He had owned a tidy
little farm with Merinos, down near Winterfield Center. Like Seth, he was thinking of raising heifers and

selling milk. Then, when Letty and Catherine were both in the family way, Josh commenced to fret.

A very learned man, one William Miller, had studied the Book of Revelations, pen in hand; and having completed endless figuring, had hit upon the exact time prophesied therein for the end of the world: the summer of 1843.

Josh warned his relatives that this would be their last summer. They had much better repent than sow their fields. There was no earthly use in helping a ewe to lamb, or planting an apple tree; for neither lamb nor tree would have time to grow.

Catherine remembered Josh pushing his dinner plate away, pounding his fists on her dining-room table. "Woe to those who are with child," he shouted, transported, "and those who give suck on that day!" His face shone. The whole prospect seemed to gratify him enormously. He had apparently forgotten present company.

Letty and Catherine looked across at one another. For the first time in their short acquaintance, they were in agreement. Theirs was the certainty of their sacred condition. God spoke to them in the voice of heart's blood, like flowing water.

But Josh could be frighteningly convincing. When his voice swelled and his fists thumped, and his small eyes gleamed glory, even Grandpa stirred uneasily. Little Harry had nightmares. And one day Catherine surprised Seth in the milkroom, frowning over Revelations, which he had spread open between two milk pans.

"You know, Cath," he said in a sheepish but troubled tone, "It's all here, six hundred and sixty-six and all, like Josh says. But there's an awful lot in here don't wash. Look at this, now." Catherine stooped under his arm to read the wee print. "If all you've got saved is twelve thousand times twelve, that's — well heck, there's that many good Christians around right now, not to mention all the ones dead! And Josh can't tell me they're all in the Other Place!" He shook his head, and slowly shut the book. "Ain't going to fret about it," he decided. "Leave it to Parson. Take it back in the house, Cath." And Seth went out to feed his sheep and lambs.

Catherine did likewise. She shoved the heavy Bible back on the parlor shelf with her mother's recipe book, and sat down to mend. Inside her, Nellie pushed and stretched.

Josh sold his farm for fifty dollars to an unbeliever. Draped in a white sheet he himself stood in the churchyard on red-lit summer evenings with a handful of converts, singing hymns; watching for the End.

The summer of 1843 proceeded in the customary way. It was, as other summers, a short, blessed season, too beautiful for Josh's rumblings to spoil. Catherine thought that God would never destroy anything so beautiful as His summer world. Apples and pears blossomed, white against blue skies. Lambs frolicked, leaping and twisting in the sunshine, foolish little packages of joyful confidence. Garden peas were shelled on doorstones. Men plowed behind horses or oxen. Children dropped seed in furrows. Later, little girls played house under arching branches; and boys fished in the pasture streams.

Letty and Catherine gave suck. They looked into their daughters' aimless, wandering eyes, and wondered about the future. But neither of them seriously doubted the existence of a future, good or bad. They gave suck, and only Letty came to woe. For she was homeless.

Meanwhile, Josh stood in the churchyard, waiting for some red sunset to explode. Evening after evening the sun set quietly, darkness fell; crickets chirped. And still the earth upheld Josh and his converts and Winterfield on its firm, maternal bosom. "It must be tomorrow night," he told his converts. "How long, O Lord, how long?"

Corn was shucked, pumpkins gathered under

shocks. Maples and elms glowed red as embers. Came a night of black frost, summer was definitely over. The world remained intact.

Josh took off his Ascension robe and went looking for work. During harvest this was no great problem. But in winter he journeyed to Northampton, and beyond.

As for Letty, she took up dressmaking. She had always been talented that way. Now she traveled with her baby daughter from house to house, designing and sewing for various families. She tended to stay longest with relatives, like Seth. Already she had stayed three months, and still she found work to do. Now she was making a summer dress for Nellie, a blue-flowered print with ruffles.

Patterns and cloth, scissors and needles, were laid out in the parlor. Through most of the winter Letty had sewed in the sitting room. But when Seth, Grandpa and Harry had moved the sitting-room stove upstairs to the bedroom, Catherine opened the folding doors to the parlor. "We will have to sit here, Lett. And poor Harry will have to saw tiny logs."

The little parlor stove stood against the chimney, smiling with its children's faces set among vines. When the sun shone in the front window the stove gleamed and twinkled. This morning it sulked — under the smiles — as gray as a granite slab. The small, cold room lay pale before the oncoming storm. On the lounge under the window Nellie and Jane sat with their samplers. At the round table, Letty struggled with a ruffle.

"Storm's a-coming," Catherine told them cheerfully. "The old cow kicked the pail and knocked Harry clean across the drain! All the stock's nerved up."

Letty bit her thread. "Tell Harry we need logs in here. What's he doing, playing Indian on snowshoes again? This room is freezing!"

Nellie twisted suddenly, dropping her sampler, and

knelt up to look out the window. "If he's on those snowshoes — "

Catherine stooped very gingerly to retrieve the sampler. "Papa made him those snowshoes for his birthday. He don't need your say-so to play with them."

"But I'm better on them than he is. Why doesn't Papa make me some too?"

"Winter's almost over. Nell" — Catherine was inspecting the sampler — "you aren't trying. This is . . ." She hesitated to say "awful" in front of prim, demure Jane, whose sampler could have graced a front hallway. But awful it was. The letters, well, you could about tell what they were. But now that Nell had started on her name, impatience and distaste danced a jig with the stitches.

There had been some discussion as to what name she should stitch. Letty voted for "Cornelia," Nellie for "Nell." "Cornelia's miles too long," she protested. "Jane's got only four letters. She'll finish way first." Jane looked up sharply at that. Catherine gave her a quick, special smile, to show she understood that Jane could have finished a month ago, that she was only holding back for Nellie.

"All right," she had decided. "Cornelia *is* too long. Nell's too short. Make it Nellie Bennett. After all, we're going to frame this under glass, and keep it forever." Now she wondered if this would be possible. Maybe it would be wisest to lose the thing and start again next fall.

"This room is freezing," Letty remarked again, around a mouthful of pins. Catherine did not answer. She had heard the crash of logs in the dining-room woodbox, and now she heard small boots stumbling across the front hall. Harry reeled in, his arms full of half-pint logs. After him came Baby Myron, staggering and laughing with a log hugged tight in his arms.

"Sure pop is cold out," Harry announced to the parlor. "West sky looks like a tombstone!" He dumped the logs in the box and helped Myron toss his in.

Catherine asked, "Are the woodboxes full?"

"Well . . ."

"We're going to need them topped off."

"I just got to get warm first." Harry pulled off his cap. Hair like sunshine spilled down his collar. He stamped his frozen feet, dancing awkwardly in front of the inefficient little heater. Chuckling, Myron danced after him. Jane giggled. Nellie pricked her finger, and exclaimed, "Cackling catfish! Harry," she called over Myron's rising shouts of joy, "I want to walk on your snowshoes today."

"Well . . ." Harry eyed her doubtfully.

"Before dinner."

"Well . . . if you're right careful."

"You know I'm better'n you!"

Catherine had to intervene. "You're good and warm, Harry, go finish your stent. Nell, you'll have to rip this out and start from the N."

But inside she laughed, joyous as little Myron. The threatening storm darkening the windows only accentuated the cheer in the untidy little parlor. Harry jammed his cap on and strode for the door, gesturing to Myron to stay back; he was working now, he couldn't be bothered with a child at his heels. Catherine grabbed Myron against Orin's bulk and hugged him. He squirmed in her arms, protesting, and she let him go quickly enough; already her arms were happy from the feel of him. She would have liked to hug Nell, too, but she restrained herself. She had the sweeping up to do, dinner to put together, bread to knead. And what was she doing standing still, listening to joy bubble within, like spring water?

Jane did not cough again till evening.

They were all gathered in the dining room, near the crackling stove. Catherine lit the astral lamp on the big, round table. This lamp, their wedding gift from Seth's parents, was the only touch of luxury in the house; and Catherine lit it, on winter evenings, with solemn ritual. Lifting the shade carefully, she set it

aside and broke a match from the sheet, then raised
the wick to meet the tiny flame. Golden light suffused
the room. She turned the light down to a comfortable
glow, returned the tasseled shade; and the household
gathered in the circle of light.

Grandpa popped corn on the stove. Letty and Catherine, at the table, leaned their knitting to the light.
Between them, Seth pored over the *Winterfield Star*.
Folding his arms across the page he dropped his nose
almost onto the letters, reading slowly, frowning and
chuckling; for the *Winterfield Star*, passed from farm
to farm, was handwritten.

Catherine said, "Letty, why don't you go up. You
look wore out."

Seth said, "Letty needs to get out of the house more.
You ought to go slide with the youngsters." Letty shot
him a bitter look. "Oh, I don't mean no harm, Lett.
Heck, I couldn't saw all day and knit all night, my
eyes would pop!"

Grandpa buttered his popcorn. Shep whined and
wagged in the back hall. He was not usually allowed
in the dining room, but Catherine saw that this was a
special occasion. There was hot popcorn on the table
— even she could smell it — and the children were
playing hide and seek through the cold front rooms.
She invited Shep in. He came timidly through the for-
bidden doorway. Myron ran and threw himself on
Shep. Myron was It.

"Go find," he babbled into the cocked ear, "Shep
go find!" Shep knew those words, though they usually
applied to sheep. He shook himself, sending golden
fluff flying over the rag rug, and trotted around the
room, poking his long nose against curtains and under
chairs while Myron urged him on.

They found Harry squeezed into the linen closet
and Nellie curled on the window seat, behind the curtains. Jane they did not find until she coughed.

She was crouched under the table, screened by
boots and skirts. Myron pulled her out, shrieking tri-

umph, while Shep wagged around them. Catherine put down her knitting.

"That's that," she declared, rising. "Remind me I'm on knit one. You're getting a good dose of sage right off."

Jane sulked. After the expected interval, she coughed again.

"You've been runnin' around like chippies," Grandpa remarked. "Wearin' yourselves out. Come and sit a minute, and I'll tell you a story."

Catherine in the kitchen heard the discussion, punctuated by coughs. "Tell about the little feet on the doorstone," Nellie suggested.

"Nah," Harry objected, "I don't wanta hear about Noah for a while. Tell about the boy with differia."

"I know!" Jane coughed, then continued: "Tell about the lilac lady." Catherine paused to listen.

All winter Jane had been insisting that there was — there really was — a lady hiding in the bushes by the road. "Wears a blue dress, braids her hair. She stands so still you can't hardly see her. Then when you do, she shrinks up and hides."

Harry would snort at this story. "A blue dress in winter? And it so cold the sheep all froze to death?"

Letty would bow closer over her sewing. Catherine suspected that she knew something about Jane, and Jane's imagination, she wasn't letting on about.

But Grandpa was moved. The first time Jane described her lady he bit his tongue. They all heard him gasp, and saw blood between his missing teeth. "That's why they talk it up," Catherine thought angrily, "to get Grandpa riled. That Jane's a mean little thing." And she forgot to sweeten Jane's dose.

"No siree," Grandpa refused calmly. "Nope. I'll tell you about Jairus' Daughter. And then it's up to bed with you, and me, too. Holy mackerel, I ain't slept a night through since sap run!" He closed his eyes, tipped back his chair, and began the story in a higher, more formal voice. "Once upon a time there was a

man named Jairus, and he had a little girl sick. So
sick he thought she'd die . . ."

A chair scraped. Seth yawned. "I'm going out to
bed the stock." He came shambling out to the kitchen,
dragging on his "sheep coat."

"Wait," said Catherine. "I'll go with you."

The milkroom was frigid, loud with the voice of
water; dark. Seth pushed aside Harry's snowshoes —
"That boy's got to learn to hang 'em up" — and
opened the back door. Snow whirled in. While corn
popped and children laughed in the lamplight, out in
the dark the storm had broken.

In the huge barn that Seth, Grandpa and the neighbors had raised in a day, the stock was warm and
quiet. Now that the storm had commenced, the nervous spell was over. Soft eyes glowed dark in the
swinging rays of Seth's lantern. Ears flicked, jaws
munched, big hoofs stamped gently. The barn smelled
cosily of feed, manure, warm bodies. Snow rattled
against the wall.

Seth went from cow to horse, doled out more hay
here, slapped a flank there. He shone the lantern into
the sheep pen. The stirring flock muttered greeting.
He looked at each balloon-sided ewe in turn, and
shook his head. "Tonight," he told Catherine, "we
can all sleep." The snow said the same, sweeping in
rhythmic waves against the wall. "Nothing going to
happen tonight — unless *you're* that way. You don't
feel that way, do you?" He sounded anxious. She re-
assured him. "Wouldn't be the best time for it," he
went on. "Bet we're snowed in, come morning. Likely
be a day or two till the team breaks out the road."

"No fear," she promised.

They walked back to the house through the fast-
deepening snow.

Letty was feeding the dining-room stove its nightly
chunk as they came in. She had soapstones heating on
top, and Baby, half asleep already, dressed in his
nightshirt. The little girls were undressing behind high-

backed chairs, giggling and whispering as they tossed
dresses and petticoats over onto the seats. "Tch-tch,"
said Letty. She arranged the clothes in neat piles.

Jane coughed, worse than before. "Did she take
her tea?" Catherine asked.

Letty gestured at the empty mug. "You forgot to
put honey," she reproached.

"I'm sorry." Catherine really was sorry when Jane
emerged in her flannels. Her normally pale, "delicate"
face was hot, her eyes dry and hard. Catherine whispered hopefully, "She doesn't have a fever?"

"She's delicate," Letty whispered. Jane heard, and
simpered most annoyingly.

Letty handed each child a hot, towel-wrapped
soapstone for the freezing sheets. "Nellie can carry
the candle." Seth swung dozing Myron to his shoulder, and Catherine snuffed the astral lamp. Darkness
swooped in from the corners. In the sleepy silence the
chunk could be heard catching fire in the stove.
Fingertips of snow drummed on the shutters. At the
head of the stairs, Jane coughed.

3

Next morning Catherine said "Nellie, do the B over." She spoke hurriedly, turning from the range on her way to the backstairs with a mustard plaster for Jane.

Nellie looked up mournfully. She leaned against the kitchen table washing the breakfast dishes. "Do I have to? I want to stay with Jane."

"Well, do it with Jane." But at the door Catherine paused. "No, don't." Apparently whatever Jane had was catching. Myron was pale this morning and had eaten no porridge. She expected him to commence coughing any moment. "No, there's no use you getting sick. Sit in the dining room, lamb, where it's warm. With Shep." Catherine dragged herself up the backstairs, Orin protesting all the way.

Letty met her in the hall. Letty had not slept all night, she looked thinner and whiter than usual, she drooped against the wall. Her eyes were pools of anxiety.

"Letty, don't upset yourself so. It's just a cold."

Letty turned and opened the door to her room. "Come see, Katie. See for yourself."

Annoyed but smiling, Catherine stomped in and stood over Jane. Letty opened the shutters. The dim room looked bitterly bleak. The walls here were as yet unplastered, fierce drafts breathed between the boards. A fringe of snow lay on the floor under the window. In her half of the tumbled bed, huddled under two quilts, Jane gasped like a caught fish. Dull, tangled hair stuck to her shrunken cheeks. Overnight, she had aged some sixty years. At sight of the mustard plaster, she strangled on a cough.

Catherine bent and felt the small, hot face, and down inside the nightdress. Hotter. Annoyance fell away from her heart, pity moved in. This delicate child was really sick.

"She oughtn't to be in here, Letty, it's too cold. Let's move her to our room, and light the stove. Thank goodness Seth has it all set up!"

Relief brightened Letty's tired eyes. She looked as Harry looked when he caught a squirrel in a neat little box trap.

The big bedroom was prepared for Orin's advent. ("Don't let it be today, Lord," Catherine prayed as she changed the sheets.) Harry brought up logs and got the fire going. Then she shooed him away. "Don't come back in here. I don't want this complaint playing dominoes with you youngsters." The room warmed, and Catherine latched the shutters tight and brought in a lamp. The cozy light glowed on rag rugs and quilts. Letty chivvied Jane out of bed, half-carried her across the hall, and dumped her in the big bed. "She looks better already."

"You sit here." Catherine pushed a rocker beside the bed. "I'll send Nellie up with your breakfast. I bet you could use some coffee."

But she did not send Nellie. She carried up the tray herself, taking the steep stairs slowly, pausing to lean against the wall and pant. The stairs had never seemed so steep.

Up and down those stairs she went all day. Medicine and fuel went up, slops came down. Catherine tried to carry the slops to the backhouse. She drew a shawl over her head and shoulders and stepped out the back door. Snow stung her face, whirling dizzily. She had to feel her way along the side of the house, which was now solid white over its red paint. When she judged she was almost at the milkroom corner a bent, thickset shadow loomed before her. A hand groped for hers, took the pail.

"Get in the house, girl," said Grandpa.

Catherine panted, "Seth?"

"Lambin'."

She fought her way back inside and collapsed at the dining-room table. "Dear Lord," she prayed silently, "don't let all this bring Orin in a hurry!" Orin kicked reassurance. As long as he moved forcefully, she knew the time was not yet.

Gradually coming to herself, she noticed Nellie. Mouse-quiet, poor Nellie sat curled in the window seat, trapped between storm outdoors and misery indoors. At her feet, Shep watched Catherine with guilty eyes.

"He can stay, Mama, can't he? It's so lonesome, without Jane!"

"He can stay." Shep's tail thumped the floor. "Nellie, did you do the B?"

"Look." Nellie slid off the window seat and brought the sampler to Catherine. The new B, still wobbly, was an improvement.

"Lovely," Catherine warbled, "lovely. Now, why don't you start the E. If you have it done by suppertime I'll show it to Jane, she won't believe her eyes."

"Mama, is Jane very sick?"

"Oh, no! It's only a little fever." Catherine wondered, as she spoke, how high that fever might go, come evening.

" 'Cause Myron is."

"What!"

"Myron upchucked his breakfast." (Myron had had

no breakfast, what could he upchuck?) "So Harry put him in his bed."

"Whose bed?"

"Harry's."

Up the stairs thumped Catherine, heart beating fit to burst, and into Harry's cold, unfinished room, where shutters banged in the wind and snow drifted in. There lay Myron, fever-hot. Harry sat beside him, telling him a story, Grandpa-fashion. "And Jesus came in and looked at her, and He said, 'I told you to get up. Get up right off and stop being dead.'"

"Harry, Myron's to go in his own bed. It's warmer there."

"But you said — "

"Myron's caught the complaint already, he can't catch it more. But I can't lift him. You get him in there."

Come nightfall, Jane's fever was dangerously high. Letty sat by her with a pot of cold water and rags. She dunked the rags in the water, wrung them out, and laid them on Jane's forehead and around her thin wrists. A few minutes later she would lift them off, hot, and dunk new ones. Catherine waddled in and out, bringing water to steam on the stove, watching Myron's fever rise. Grandpa dunked rags for him, and kept the steam going, so that Catherine could finally roll into Letty's cold bed and rest.

Sometime in the night she heard voices across the hall.

"That doctor," Letty was saying. "The new one, Dr. . . ."

"Peters," said Grandpa. He spoke softly, soothingly.

Letty's voice rose. "Can't we reach him?"

"Don't see how."

"Surely Seth's big Dobbin could get through — "

"Don't see how. It's gaskin-deep all the way. Deeper in the hollows."

"Mr. Bennett, are we really trapped here?"

"Yes, ma'am."

A patter of bare feet, a door opening. "Grandpa."

"Nell Baby, don't you come in here. Your mama said — "

"Is Jane very sick?"

"Fever's always high at night."

"I heard you talking 'bout the doctor. I know the way to his house."

"I know the way to China, too. Go to bed, Baby, before you catch your death."

Catherine raised herself on an elbow and shouted, "Cornelia Ann Bennett, go to bed!"

After that was silence, save for the rustle of snow against the window.

In the morning they tried to have breakfast. Catherine did not bother to set the dining-room table. She put leftovers and coffee on the kitchen table. Grandpa and Letty, exhausted, came down from the sickroom. Seth and Harry blew in the back door with a cloud of snow. Seth had been out with the ewes all night. Catherine watched him comb his hair at the shelf, moving slowly, lifting his muscular arm with tired decision.

"Coffee this morning." She poured him a mugful.

"I drink tea in the morning." He dropped into his chair.

"Coffee'll do you good."

Seth drew his plate toward him. It was heaped high with potluck dinner. "How are the invalids?"

Letty wept.

Catherine laid a hand over Letty's chilly claw. With her free hand, Letty pulled a fever rag out of her apron pocket and buried her face in it. Nellie watched, blue eyes trouble-darkened over the rim of her mug. She was drinking coffee too, because Catherine was too bothered to notice.

Grandpa said, "Fever lets down toward mornin'. 'Course, it'll likely go higher as the day progresses."

Seth laid down his knife. He looked from Catherine to Grandpa. "Girl's throat swollen?"

"Ayah." Grandpa nodded. "Raspberries."

"White spots?"

From behind the coffeepot Harry said clearly, "White spots, differia."

Letty howled. Catherine rose and embraced her, petted her shoulders, caressed her coarse, unbrushed hair. "No, no," she soothed. "Harry, don't say a word like that. It's just a bad cold, Seth. No spots."

"Did you look?"

"We'd have seen — "

Seth stood up. His chair tipped and crashed over, and no one moved to pick it up. "I'm going up and look. If there's white spots I'm getting to that doctor if I have to fly." He stepped over the chair and strode into the backhall. They heard him thud up the stairs.

Harry said, "I'll go, on my snowshoes."

Catherine clasped Letty's head between her firming breasts. At this moment she noticed the ache in them. ("Not yet, dear Lord, not yet!") "Don't talk like that, Harry. You say such awful things — "

"Why's that awful? I bet I could — "

"Harry! You couldn't even see where you were going! Now be quiet, eat your breakfast." And to Letty, "Shh, shhh."

By the time Seth returned, a tense order was restored. He picked up his chair, plunked himself down, and went to work on the potluck.

Grandpa prodded. "Well?"

"Don't know for sure. Girl wouldn't let me look. Myron's got no spots, I know that."

Catherine's throat relaxed. "Then I take it you don't have to fly?"

"Huh? Oh. Not yet a while." Seth ate hungrily now, already reaching for more.

Catherine eased her bulk down and poured herself another mug. "I don't know why I'm drinking this, I must be the only one slept last night! Nellie, why don't you spend the morning doing the N." Anxiously, she watched Nellie eat. The child showed no signs of complaint now, but this thing moved fast. "You feel good, Nell?"

"Yes'm. Can I be with Jane?"

. . "No, lamb."

Nellie sighed. "Morning takes forever without Jane."

Morning. Catherine looked at the window, so frosted and snow-beaten it was opaque. She felt the cold seeping through the walls, lingering in corners, besieging the stoves. This promised to be a long morning, perhaps the longest of her life. Upstairs, Myron cried.

"I'll look in on him," Grandpa said, getting up. "I'm goin' up to bed anyhow. Set a while, Catherine, drink your coffee. Do you a world of good."

4

"Mama!" Jane cried to Catherine, "Take the snake away!" She pointed, her face contorted with horror. Catherine picked at the quilt where Jane pointed, pretended to lift and throw. "It's gone, dear, see." Jane moaned, and hid under the bedclothes.

From the trundle bed sounded Myron's whimpers and gasps; and Seth's whispered prayer. Turning to dunk Jane's hot cloth in cold water, Catherine glimpsed Seth bent across the dim light. Elbows planted on each side of Myron's small, twisting form, he clasped heavy hands and bowed his head, whispering, "Out of the depths have I cried unto thee."

"Lord, hear my prayer," Catherine breathed.

As Grandpa had warned, the fevers had grown with the day. Now in the early night both children were surely the sickest they could be? Cathrine rubbed her eyes with cold water. Darkness and lurking cold and the drumming of snow on the shutters had been her world forever. If she tried to lift herself out of this, to imagine summer, or sunshine, or everybody laughing together after supper, the images seemed unreal, fantastic; like the old fairy tales Grandpa sometimes told. Her sense of reality was further weakened by exhaustion. She had sent Letty to bed across the hall. Grandpa had slept all day, then gone to the sheep. While the grownups slept in snatches, and took turns in the steam-misted, sick-smelling bedroom, Harry and Nellie wandered like ghosts, forgotten.

Nellie said from the doorway, "Jane called you 'Mama.'"

Catherine rounded on her slowly. "Stay out," she replied automatically. Spreading the cloth in the icy water, she noticed Nellie's strained, tense little face, the eyes huge and shadowed under a mane of snarls. "Please the Lord, you're not feeling sick?"

"No'm, I'm fine." Here it must be ten o'clock, and Nellie still dressed, still wandering the cold house! Catherine sighed, and pressed the cloth to her eyes before replacing it on Jane's wrist. "Nellie, go to bed."

"I want to pray with Papa."

Seth raised his head from his hands. "Go pray by yourself, Nell. The Lord can hear you just as good in your own room."

"You want I should pray, Papa?"

"Pray. By all means."

Nellie went away. Catherine dozed; started up;

changed the water. They kept three basins in the
room: one by Jane, one by Myron, and one on the sill,
where the water froze. To replenish Jane's basin,
Catherine broke ice.

The wind moaned like a sick child. The old house
seemed to sway. Furtive footsteps creaked in the hall,
on the stairs. Rats rustled in the walls. Toward morning Catherine slept, slumped in her chair.

She was jerked awake by a foot punching her stomach. A small hand fluttered, inside. She remembered
Orin. "So there is a future," she thought, surprised.

And the future was moving rapidly into the present.
There was a difference. She opened her eyes, lifted
her head cautiously, not to break her stiff neck. The
difference was silence.

No snow rattled against the house. No shutters
swung. From the beds, no moans or whimpers; just
steady, gentle breathing.

Catherine leaned forward, studying Jane in the dim
light of the failing lamp. Jane lay quietly on her side.
One skeletal little hand lay flung outside the quilt.
Catherine touched it, reached around its wrist; cool.

She rose, set her chair aside softly, leaned over the
trundle bed. Myron slept. His breaths came soft and
sweet, tiny flowers of breaths. Beside him Seth
sprawled in his chair, chin sunk in his chest, big hands
still clasped. He had dozed in the midst of prayer.

"Fever always lets down, come mornin'." Catherine
heard Grandpa saying it. But this letdown was real,
she knew. Later, the children would be sick again, but
not that sick. They were out of danger.

Only now could she let herself think about that danger.

Very gently she moved outside the room, silently
shut the door. She went to the window at the front of
the hall and opened the shutters. The window was
snow-paned, yet daylight looked through it. Daylight
stole into the hall, touched the blue-stenciled walls,
blessed the top step of the front stairway. The house

slept, breathing gently under the soothing hand of light.

"The Lord heard my prayer," Catherine thought, "and let my cry come unto Him." The silent house vibrated unconscious relief. It was a happy house — but cold. Death had passed by. Now Life hesitated. Catherine squeaked open Harry's door, poked her head inside. "I'm going down, Harry," she said softly to the darkness. "You better get up, and look spry about it." Cows must be milked, wood split, fires stirred, as though nothing wonderful had happened.

"Uuuuu," said Harry. The bed creaked.

"And, Harry. We're all right."

"Uuuuu?" His voice came clearer, he had lifted his head. "Myron's all right?"

"Yes, dear. We're all of us all right."

In the kitchen she poked up the fire, drew the teapot forward onto the heat, and looked about for Shep. He should be wagging at the door, now, wanting to go out. "Hey, Shep!" He should thump his tail in answer, even if he were too sleepy yet to move. "I'm going out, Shep. You better come too." No answer. She went to the backhouse without him.

The morning was quiet, cold, resting. A few snow-flakes still spiraled down through pearly air. In the west the sky was clearing, a blue streak widened over the barn roof. Catherine waded hip-deep to the back-house, along a vague, blown path that Harry had somehow kept shoveled. Back in the fast-warming kitchen she stamped and brushed off loose snow, and stood close to the range.

Harry barged through, heading for the milkroom and barn. He pulled his cap down over his corn-silk hair and stumbled on a flying shoelace. "I'm going to the barn on snowshoes," he cried excitedly. "Bet I can't get there without!"

"That's a good idea." Catherine went to work on her face and hair before the wavery little mirror. Her hair had not been brushed in . . . two days? She let her aching arms drop, thinking, "Letty will help me."

Unexpectedly, Harry came back from the milk-room. "Mama, have you seen my snowshoes?"

"No dear, I haven't been snow-walking lately. Papa may have hung them up for you."

"I hung them up last night, and now they're gone."

"Reckon you'll have to walk like the rest of us mortals." She turned to set the table. But the table was a mess of debris. Mugs, dishes, crumbs, spills, and Nellie's sampler were all tied together by strings of abandoned embroidery thread. "Gracious, what a mess! Look what happens in the house, do I turn my back for a minute! Harry don't fuss about your snowshoes now. The woodboxes are empty."

She picked up the sampler; NELLIE BEN in red and blue; tear-stained, blood-stained, crooked. "Tch-tch-tch," said Catherine, Lefty-fashion, and tossed the cloth over on the dresser. This calamity would certainly never be framed.

Harry noticed her motion, and the flying embroidery. "It's Nellie done it," he cried, real anger cutting his voice. "I'm gonna give her a piece of my mind!"

"Harry — "

But he was gone. She heard him rush up the back-stairs. In a minute now he would have Seth and Letty awake, with his banging around and shouting. No matter. They would wake to daylight; relief; joy.

Humming a grateful hymn, Catherine set about cleaning up. She wielded broom and dustrag, sorted out the mess, poured herself a mug of tea. Sunshine brightened the window; and presently the room took on its familiar look of shabby comfort. Catherine sank down at the table, sipped warmth, smiled at the light strengthening along the bare, plastered wall.

Harry thundered downstairs and through the front rooms. He appeared at the kitchen door, out of breath. He said, "Nell ain't upstairs."

"Harry, you forget about Nellie for now. In five minutes this room will commence to be *cold*."

"Mama. Nellie ain't upstairs. She ain't in front. She ain't nowhere." A strange, adult note of exasperated patience in his voice penetrated Catherine's euphoria. She set her mug down and looked across the clean table, along the daylit wall, at Harry. His eyes were troubled. His small, masculine hand, splayed against the doorframe, trembled. "Nellie's gone," he said. "And my snowshoes are gone. And Mama, have you seen Shep?"

5

"You don't feel nothin'. You drift off to sleep is all. There was roses all the time, and organ music, beautiful. Tell the truth, I didn't much care to come back."

An old-timer, fished out of the snow in Catherine's childhood, had told his rescuers that. And he said that you see your life pass before you, like a vanishing dream.

What dreams flowed through the little girl's dimming mind? Did she remember, perhaps, the angle of morning light across the stairs? Or Shep's head, golden on the brown rag rug? Did she remember drying the chipped stoneware dishes and stacking them on the dresser?

When you are little; when your chin rests comfortably on the dining room table; then the house is an enormous palace, table legs are trees, grownups giants. A buff of dust under a chair is thick to you, silvery, soft to touch. Floating away, Nellie must have remembered things Catherine never even noticed.

Or perhaps the old-timer was wrong. Perhaps at the end one wakes from the dream of roses and music, one realizes, and tries to struggle clear of the snow. A child might weep tears of terror that would freeze on her cheeks.

Catherine started up. Instantly faces turned, skirts rustled. Letty hurried to her side. "Nothing yet, Katie."

Old Mrs. Cook croaked, "Tell her there's still hope."

"But there's still hope." Mechanically, Letty patted Catherine's shoulders.

She sank down again at the dining-room table. Afternoon light gilded the wood along the grain. She was conscious of that, and of the hunched looming of her shadow; and of Nellie's frozen tears.

There was bustle behind and around her. Women came and went — those who lived near enough to struggle along the unbroken road, lugging pots and sacks of food, leaving their little children safe at home with Grandmother or the hired girl. Old Mrs. Cook was loudly in charge. Amy Partridge was down cellar, rummaging out potatoes and carrots to cook for the search party. Mrs. Graves, Mrs. Little and Mrs. Stone helped Letty in the kitchen. Mrs. Little's Nancy sat in the sunny window seat, rocking Myron on her lap. He whimpered and fretted, his fever dragged on miserably. Nancy crooned little songs and played pattycake, and showed him the search party on the hill. "Look, Myron, that's your papa in the blue cap. And that's my papa, with the rake. Oh! Did you see, Baby? Your brother went in up to his neck!" Nancy was the most truly helpful neighbor in the house.

Late in the day she raised a cry. Setting Myron

down among the cushions she knelt upright, waved, called out. Catherine tensed, jerked around. For a moment she thought "Nellie is found!" It was well she did not believe it. The next second she understood the cry. "Road's broken out!" Mrs. Little and Mrs. Graves hurried in from the kitchen, Amy Partridge pulled back the curtain. Even Catherine rose slowly, moved heavily to look out.

Squinting across the rosy, diamond sparkle down toward the road, she saw the town oxteam approaching, the crew shouting and waving like long-awaited rescuers; which, indeed, they were. Behind the stoneboat the road was now visible, a path of packed snow through soft snow. The oxen strained, bowing and tossing their horned heads, knotting neck muscles like thick ropes. Step by slow step they advanced, pushing snow aside with their great chests like the prows of victorious ships. The men steered by guess between the maple-lines. There was no other indication, in the wide snowscape, of where the road should be.

Outside the house the team halted. A boy stayed with the oxen. The town crew came floundering up the bank, making for the kitchen and the hot tea Catherine always had ready for them.

Dully she watched them struggle past the window, laughing and waving, surprised to see all the women inside. Amy dropped the curtain back in place. Catherine heard the stomp of boots, and voices in the kitchen. Letty must have made the tea, she heard the thump of mugs on the table.

Appreciative voices rose, loud with cold air and exertion; then softened. Near silence followed, interrupted by questioning murmurs, soft answers.

The crew drank their tea much faster than usual and departed. Catherine watched them go down past the window, sobered. Two of them — Mr. Fiske and Mr. Flower — struck off the other way, up the long hill.

She watched them join the search party. Red and

brown splotches in the sparkling white ocean, they bobbed and bowed, drew together, spread apart. Tiny in the white immensity each man fought his way through the snow, feeling around, poking with rake, hoe or shovel. "Talk about a needle in a haystack!" Mrs. Cook said loudly in the kitchen.

Catherine returned to the dining-room table. She sank down and rested her head in her hands. Wrapped in her own darkness, she prayed.

As the day faded, Letty came to light the astral lamp. Catherine watched her lift off the shade, set it gently aside, break a match from the sheet. Her eyes followed the lean, worn hands back and forth across the white apron; so many little motions, careful gestures, which she herself performed but could not have numbered or described. Flame fluttered at the wick. The alien fingers fumbled, the light turned high, then dimmed. Now the shade, delicately set down, tassels swinging, shadows swinging.

Catherine meant to look, or nod, thanks. But as she raised her eyes from Letty's hands, Jane's face pushed into the new light.

So pale this little face, it looked like a paper mask. The eyes were black holes, scissors-cut. Jane's lank hair hung flat, without braid or ribbon, though someone had taken time to comb it. Weakly she leaned against Letty. And Catherine watched with hating pain as Letty drew the child close, smoothed her hair, and whispered in her ear.

Jane nodded. Slowly, but willingly, she pushed off from Letty, gripped the edge of the table, and came edging around toward Catherine. Letty had whispered, "Kiss Aunt Katie goodnight." Another moment, and Catherine would feel small arms around her neck!

She exerted herself. She moved, drawing back from the threatened embrace. And she opened her eyes wide at Jane, letting the hate in them glow.

Jane hesitated, leaned against the table. She appealed back to Letty. Letty nodded. Jane turned away, and tottered toward the shadowed stairs. Catherine relaxed heavily.

After dark the men came in. Worn out, they flopped around the kitchen while their wives dished up beans, pot-luck and pie.

"Most like never got that far," they said.

" — Better hunt closer to home — "

" — Might have gone clear the other way, across the road — "

" — That's downhill, she'd know — "

" — Dark, snow blowin'. Couldn't tell — "

Seth brought his beans and sat with Catherine. Grief did not mark his face. All Catherine read there was tiredness. Bitterly she envied him. Caught up in action, he had not yet faced horror. When he did, it would be already familiar.

His hand sought hers on the table. She felt its hardness, the tough tightness of skin. She wondered if he could even feel the pressure of her fingers against his calloused palm. Pushing his dish away, he asked, "You ain't coming?"

She did not understand at first. "Coming? Oh! No."

He meant Orin; Orin, whom she had entirely forgotten. So still he had lain all day, she could not remember if he had kicked at all.

"Glad to hear." Seth squeezed her hand, laid his head on his arm, appeared to sleep. Harry came in. All day he had hunted with the men, floundering in snow to his armpits.

"Harry," Catherine cried, "you must go to bed!" Seth opened an eye.

Harry said, "I'm going, Mama." And suddenly he came to Catherine and hugged her, and rested his head on her shoulder, as he had not done for months now, perhaps a year. She whispered, "You did fine, Harry."

Harry dragged himself upstairs. Seth raised his head. "If you're awake and talking," he said, "we've got some good neighbors in there." He nodded toward the kitchen.

Together they rose and crossed the hall.

Grandpa sat with the men, all making feeble efforts at mutual encouragement. The women cleared away, packed leftovers, found boots and shawls.

"Back at first light," Mr. Little promised.

"Bring my dogs," Mr. Partridge suggested. "Might be scent."

Mr. Fiske mentioned the new neighbor, Dr. Peters. "I'll stop by his place, get him to come,"

"Not Dr. Peters," Catherine said. Her voice rang harsh. They all turned to look at her.

Old Mrs. Cook, tying her cloak, said sharply, "Don't do to hold grudges, Mrs. Bennett."

Amy looked up from her boot. "Ain't Doctor's fault, you know."

Catherine gripped the table. "My little girl was going . . . to see him . . . to his house. He told her where it was."

Arms came around her. "Katie! You might as well blame Jane for being sick!" Catherine looked into Letty's face. Letty's arms dropped.

Grandpa explained to the uncomfortable silence, "Catherine don't feel herself right now." With sympathetic-censorious murmurs, the crowd moved to the door.

All night lanterns crisscrossed the snowflakes close to the house. Seth went out, and the town crew, who returned after the roads were packed. Letty tended the coffeepot. Candle in hand, Catherine wandered around the dark house.

She hovered over Myron's trundle bed. Myron was frightened by the confused noises, strange voices, the tense misery he sensed all around him.

"Want Papa."

"Papa's outside, lamb. What is it? Maybe Mama can help."

Myron rolled his head, firm negation. "Want Papa!" He pushed his thumb into his mouth.

Gently, Catherine removed it. "You can't see Papa right off, Baby. You can't always see people when you want them." Released, the thumb shot back into the mouth.

"I know," said a voice from the big bed. "Myron wants a story. I'll tell you a story, Baby. Want me to?"

Startled, Catherine raised the candle. The light caught Jane, resting on one elbow, tugging Catherine's quilt over her shoulder. "Mama said to come here, Aunt Katie," she explained. Catherine managed to murmur, "Good idea. Warmer."

She left them talking softly, and carried her candle to Nellie's room. Here she stood deliberately in the draft by the shuttered window. Shaking, teeth chattering, she sheltered the candle behind her bulk. Slowly she shone the light around the bare little room. The narrow bed was unmade, the blankets tossed back, as Nellie had left them when she jumped out on the braided rug and snatched her flannels off the chair . . . Unless, perhaps, she had slept in flannels? Then she had sneaked past the room where Catherine, bent over Jane, was too concerned to hear the little feet in the hall, on the stairs. Down in the warm dining room Nellie had pulled on dress and shoes; then on to the kitchen, to feel for the coat hanging behind the door . . . and out to the milkroom, past the cold gurgle of magic, never-frozen water. She would have to strain on tiptoe to lift Harry's snowshoes down. And here, perhaps, she would begin to shiver, even hesitate?

"Come, Shep. Shep, let's go out." Even a grownup, frantic with anxiety, would hesitate to face the freezing dark alone!

But a grownup would know. When Letty had suggested going for Dr. Peters, Grandpa had said firmly, "Don't see how." A grownup would recognize Impossibility. It needed the ignorance of a stubborn child to push the door open, leaning against the weight of snowy wind.

"Katie! Heavens, you don't want to catch your death *now!*" In the open door Letty's face appeared, lit momentarily by a flickering candle which the cold draft snuffed. Firmly she came across the uneven floor, took Catherine by the arm, drew her out of the room. They passed the bedroom door where Jane tiredly held forth: "So Jesus went upstairs and looked at the little dead girl, and He told all the people 'She ain't dead. She's asleep.'"

Lantern light crossed and recrossed the front-hall window. Men were searching down by the road. Circles of light swung among the naked lilacs.

"The girl is not dead," Catherine whispered, "but sleeping." Such things happened in stories. In a story, a child could sleep under snow, wrapped in a sheep dog's warmth, through two nights and a day.

6

Warm sunset light slanted across the window seat. Patched cushions glowed like jewels. Gold dust floated. Glancing quickly, Catherine thought she saw a small form half hidden behind the curtain and sucking a pricked finger.

She hurried away into the living room, half-consciously seeking the coldest parts of the house. Cold, she felt closer to her lost child.

Thus seeking cold and uncomfort she came to the parlor. The door of the little stove yawned open. Catherine set it shut, and the children's faces smiled at her. She recognized them. They were all one chubby little girl, maybe seven years old.

Quickly she looked away from the faces, at the dusty disorder reigning here, in what should be a sanctuary of grave tidiness. Letty's sewing lay heaped on the table, bristling with needles, threads dangling. Topmost lay a little blue dress, ruffled, with pockets. Here was no sanctuary, no help. "Better neaten up," she thought, "for the funeral." For now it was three days, and three nights.

Now there was no longer hope. It was simply a matter of finding the . . . remains. Somewhere under the snow a breathless thing waited for the touch of rake or hoe. Until it was found, Catherine did not see how she could take up her life again. Other people were already doing this. Grandpa went about his and Seth's chores steadily, only a trifle more gray and bent than before. Letty busied herself with Myron and Jane, and with meals for the helpful neighbors. The women kept the house cleaner than Catherine usually did, and watched through the windows while their husbands toiled in the snow.

For five hundred yards around the house the snow was churned like butter, every square foot poked and stomped. Beyond, there were still virgin vistas. The men broke new trails, every hour higher on the hill. With forlorn pride, Catherine thought that Nellie might have gone much farther than the men thought possible. She might have gone clear over the hill.

That night the men said, "We'll know when it melts." They downed the last tea and called to their wives. They were giving up. Catherine looked from one exhausted, red-splotched face to another, and managed to thank them all.

"Hope we can do as much for you," Seth said formally. "I don't mean just that," he amended hastily, "I mean . . . thank you."

"You can't blame them," he said to Catherine in bed. "George Little has the store to tend, Abner Fiske's got the mill. Everybody has to look to his stock, or business, whatever. It ain't as if . . ." He did not finish. It was not, after all, as though there were hope.

Catherine could not blame the neighbors. But she almost blamed Seth when she heard him sleeping. How could he sleep while his daughter's remains lay under the snow! With a determined effort at understanding, she realized that this was his first night in bed for . . . three nights. She had not been in bed either, but she had sat around, rested on the lounge, napped sometimes on Nellie's narrow bed. Nor had she floundered, day and night, in waist-high snow.

In the hard circle of Seth's arm, warm against his relaxed length, Catherine drifted into guilty sleep. She wandered in a storm. Snow stung her face. Snow attacked, dizzying, from all quarters. She turned right and left and right around, only to meet flying snow. Gratefully, she stepped on something unsnow; something hard, that sounded under her step.

She stood back and looked at it. Brushing snow off it with her shoe, she saw it was a wooden plank; a door, leading down; a trapdoor.

"No," said Catherine.

The trapdoor dropped. Soundlessly it fell away into unguessed deeps of darkness. And Catherine's feet moved forward, as they had to. There was no stopping, no drawing back. Relentless as time, the snow-wind pushed her toward the edge. She grabbed at hurtling snowflakes; cried out; and fell.

Seth's arm jerked tight around her. Her eyes opened, staring into night.

"You all right?"

"Ayah."

"You coming?"

"Not a while. Go to sleep if you can."

He could. In a few moments his arm relaxed. His breath passed, warm and regular, down her neck.

A cold hand gripped the end of Catherine's spine, and squeezed. The chill pain held, strengthened, faded. She counted slowly to one hundred, before the fingers of pain tightened again on her spine.

One hundred. "Yet a while off," she thought. No need to rouse Seth. But it was certainly beginning. "This time tomorrow I'll see his face." Orin's new face would be red and wrinkled, smaller than the palm of her hand. But he would have his own look, stamped upon him long before his entry to the outer world. He would look like Orin, not like Grandpa, or Seth, or Seth's mother Jenny, or herself, no matter what polite visitors might exclaim. Traces of all these faces would be found in his; but Orin would be Orin.

"Or Alma, of course." From the beginning she had imagined Orin masculine; but she might be mistaken. Deliberately, she prepared to love.

Icy fingers fumbled, found her spine, squeezed. The trapdoor was there before her. As the pain strengthened, gathered force, and suddenly diminished, Catherine began to remember what lay beneath the door.

One skated over the crust of life; one flew, resting only momentarily on any portion of the brittle surface. Pause too long, hesitate, and one could fall through into hell.

Fed, you find it hard to imagine hunger. Warm, you can only wonder how it feels to freeze. Healthy, you sympathize with the sick — it *is* too bad, and would you like some nice sage tea? — but you cannot feel the fever-chill till it happens in your own bones. And then you cannot describe it. And afterwards you cannot remember.

But now, tutored by the gripping pains that came at intervals of one hundred, ninety-five, ninety, Catherine remembered. Holding her breath at the height of a pain, gritting her teeth, she began to smile. Falling slowly through the trapdoor of pain one leaves the world behind; and all guilt, and failure.

When the rooster crowed out in the barn, and gray light stole across the trundle bed, the cradle and piled diapers, Catherine inched out of bed. She had time to start the day right before calling Seth. She would have the kettle boiling, the house warm. Downstairs, she found no water in the kettle. She took it to the milk-room.

The door closed behind her. The house was shut out, with all its necessities and urgencies and pro-fusion of remorse-colored things. Alone in the dim-ness, Catherine was washed in the sound of water.

Slowly she waddled forward, toward the shaft of tumbling light that slithered through the wall and down the trough. Gurgling, the water spilled into the tub, where it deepened in silence. Catherine took up the dipper and leaned over. Shadows swirled in the water. Eddies whispered. Catherine dipped and drank, and pure coldness burned her throat.

The dipper dropped into the tub. Circling, it filled and sank. Catherine pushed up her sleeves and dived after it. Her arms were pillars of ice, her dress soaked through, ice seemed to melt on her hot, hard breasts. Still the dipper eluded her reach. Straightening, she waited while a pain attacked, took over, lessened.

Then she pushed her sleeves to the shoulders, lifted water in cupped hands, and sloshed her face. Frigid streams filled her eyes, ran down her neck. She took a deep breath, reached far down for the dipper, drew it up and drank greedily, before filling the kettle.

She knew again, "I am alive." And falling slowly back to the reality of herself and her situation that morning, she knew for a blessed moment that she had been there again, in the heart of creation, at the foun-tain of secret joy.

She leaned as far over the rim as Orin would let her. Her reflection was broken, and ringed and rippled among water-shadows. She said aloud. "Josh

Bennett! I see you, down there! Did you think the world had ended?"

Vigorous hands took her shoulders, turned her around. She rested her head on Seth's chest. "You all right?"

"I'm all right." She realized the reality of Seth. He was bigger than she, and firmer, if not as round. His heart thumped in her ear. "Seth, are *you* all right?"

"Me! I'm not the one birthing!" She tightened her arms around him. Between them, Orin rolled over.

"Seth. Do something for me. Something I can't do, just yet."

"What's that?"

"You know the dress Letty was making for . . . ? The blue one. Tell her she can have it for Jane. She can take it in to fit."

"I'd feel kind of peculiar, saying that."

"I wish you would, Seth."

"All right, I will."

"And then you can harness Big Dobbin, go for Mrs. Pease."

"It's time?"

"Nigh on."

As she spoke into his neck; gripping him in trembling arms; the trapdoor opened under her feet.

The Cocoon 1900

I celebrate myself.
—*Walt Whitman*

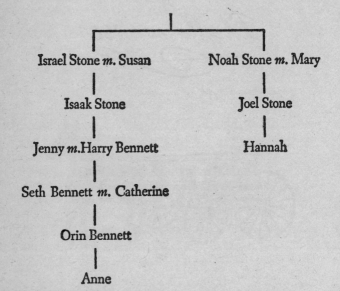

Israel Stone *m.* Susan   Noah Stone *m.* Mary

Isaak Stone   Joel Stone

Jenny *m.* Harry Bennett   Hannah

Seth Bennett *m.* Catherine

Orin Bennett

Anne

1

So bright was that autumn, the dooryard maple flushed red as the newly painted house. Against an intense, deep sky leaves drifted continuously, a shower of gold. (Very privately, in her Very Secret Journal, Anne Bennett called this season the "Time of Danaë.") Most years, the golden shower lasted through ten perfectly incredible days; days when even Anne's mother, down-to-earth Mrs. Bennett, born and raised in a hill town, would stand on the doorstone for minutes on end, staring up and out into glory. This year the shower went on and on. Day after luminous day gold drifted in and out of maple-shadows along the road. Anne sneaked her Very Secret Journal out from under her best petticoats in the top drawer — a hiding place known only to herself and her twin sister — and wrote, "Bennett Road is paved with gold."

In a less poetic vein, her father, Orin Bennett, said the same. "You want a new dress, Anne? Katie, you still hankering for mohair tops? Now's the time. We're made of gold!"

The farm year had been remarkably successful. Calves thrived, feed crops doubled their yield, milk prices held. From the hay-stuffed barn to the spring and beyond, pastures and mowings were still richly green. "How about that foulard, Mother, with all the flounces?" Orin smiled about at his family, gathered at the breakfast table. Leaning back, he swelled his chest slightly and plucked at his overall straps with calloused, blunt thumbs.

Mrs. Bennett set before him an apple pie, swimming in cream. "We can do better than that, Orin," she said, sitting down and shaking out her napkin. "Clothes and shoes are all very well, but as I see it, the real tug-of-war is between the new icebox, and . . ." She glanced at her daughters. They were busily passing butter, cream, salt; Orin, who really wanted the foolish thing, still teetered, fiddling with his straps. He was waiting for her to say it. Very well. "What we've been kind of thinking about all summer. You know. The parlor organ."

Orin set his chair down on all four legs and took up his fork. "Remember what they said in town meetin' about the chandelier: 'Before we buy one, let's be sure someone knows how to play it!' "

No one laughed. Orin had been peddling that joke for six months. Katie said, "Syrup please? We can learn how after we get one. Aunt Alma would love to teach us." This did elicit smiles, and muffled laughter. They laughed kindly at Aunt Alma, whose amateur musical career was a family joke; and they laughed with joy at the prospect of a real parlor organ, concrete, sonorous, paid for. It would occupy the space by the divan, now filled by a phantom wish-organ.

They bought organ and icebox, foulard and mohair tops; and still Orin looked for a way to share prosperity and gladden his womenfolk. An idea hit him the day the hired men topped off the cornercrib. "It would take days to husk that crop," he said proudly. "We'll do it in an hour! We'll give a bee!"

Word was out around town next morning. Mrs. Bennett told Central, who relayed the news wherever a telephone rang; and Anne told her pupils at the Center School, who told brothers and sisters, who told friends, "Husking bee at Bennetts! And Mrs. Bennett makes the best doughnuts in town!"

"How many do we expect?" Mrs. Bennett asked, the morning of the bee. Orin opined that "twenty dozen ought to hold them."

"We'll do eight." Mrs. Bennett tied on her brown pinafore, knotted a kerchief over her gray hair, and poked up a hot fire in the range. "Leave the door open to breathe!"

"You'll have flies in here, Mama," Anne warned. For flies still buzzed in the autumn sunshine.

Her mother set out the heavy board and rolling pin, boughten flour and homemade baking powder. "Too hot in here for flies! Trot to the pantry, Annie, fetch me the cream. Katie, love, see if there aren't some eggs behind the mower."

Like the good little girls their mother still saw in them the twins hurried to obey. Shortly Anne returned from the watercooled pantry, the cream in the full pitcher trembling to her firm step. Katie tripped in flushed with exertion, straw in her bright hair, her apron full of brown eggs. "They've found a new nest. This one's under the tack."

Orin panted up from the cellar with the cider jug. "You two hang lanterns — and make double sure there's no hay near or under!"

The sisters went out to the barn; and Mrs. Bennett, breaking eggs, murmured, "Do them good, maybe, to do something together."

Surprised, Orin turned to her. "Do something together! They've done everything together since they were knee-high to — "

"Not lately. Haven't you noticed?"

"Oh. That. That ain't serious. Is it?"

"It's getting there, Orin."

"Mmmm. Was this bee the best idea then, do you think? In that case?"

Stirring the eggs in, she nodded. "Bring it to a head."

Anne trimmed wicks on the half-wall of the horse stall. As she reset each lantern, Katie hung it from a beam above the clear-swept circle. Sunshine flooded in through the great doors, and with sunshine, the cheerful chirp of crickets. But the twins maintained a strained, cold silence.

Anne glanced from Katie's waiting hands to her pretty face, framed in sunny curls and topped with a ribbon. "I could be that pretty," she thought. "Goodness, I *am* that pretty!" For Katie's face was her own; or almost. A softer, lighter spirit — what Anne considered a more "feminine" spirit — looked out of Katie's gray eyes. Anne could not conceal the essential gravity of her studious soul. Nevertheless, "If I took my hair down and curled it, and pressed a ribbon, I would be every bit that pretty. And Ernest knows it." She had seen the knowledge in his eyes.

Katie took the lantern Anne had set aside and climbed the stepladder. Her little feet twinkled under the swinging skirt. She balanced on top like a butterfly, fluttering. A month ago, Anne would have rushed to steady the ladder. Now, she watched calmly from the half-wall. Unassisted, Katie found her balance, hung the lantern, and climbed down gingerly. "Don't break your neck, Sis, running to help!"

"I knew you'd make it," Anne said quietly.

"You can say that again!" Katie nodded vigorously, giving the words emphatic meaning. "You can just say that again! I always make it, every time. I don't need *your* help."

Later, with the hired men, they heaped corn in the middle of the lantern circle, and placed baskets around. Anne murmured to Katie, "How many red ears, do you think?" Feeling guilty about the ladder incident, she came up behind Katie and murmured into her ear, as of old.

Katie refused the olive branch. "No twin ears," she said loudly, "only singles." The hired men glanced up, then pretended they had not heard.

"But a fellow might get *two* single red ears, mightn't he? He might even kiss two different girls! It's not a proposal, you know, it's a . . . game."

"Many a jest is said in earnest." And Katie swished purposefully away to the other side of the growing pile of corn.

Later in the morning, Mrs. Bennett discovered a sugar shortage. "I didn't expect no bee, of course; but even so, I can't think how I come to run so low! Annie, would you drive to Little's for me?"

It was a morning to be out of doors, away from Katie. Happy's dainty hoofs thudded softly on the dirt road. Glad to be trotting through the bright morning, she flicked her tail and blew; spittle drifted back and sprayed Anne's face. Faster plunked the hoofs, wheels rumbled, pebbles flew. Happy's glossy chestnut rump bumped along, her mane flopped; the buggy rolled through maple-shade, gold-showered.

Anne held the reins loose in one firm hand; with the other she held down her bouncing hat. Shaken, and a trifle bruised where she had knocked against the guard, she was still elated. The farther they bumped away from the red farmhouse, the higher rose her spirits. Very rarely did she drive by herself like this. Usually Katie sat beside her, laughing and gossiping — though not of late; or her mother, plump hands folded in her jiggling lap or if any man were present, of course *he* drove. But Anne loved to drive. She loved the feeling of power and speed, wind in her face; she loved Happy's willing strength; she loved the farmhouses rising out of fields and sinking behind stone walls, the shade trees flashing by, sun-speckled. She loved the world.

At the head of the steep downturn she had to draw

rein. "Slow," she called to Happy. "Waaalk." Happy turned back her ears, blew, slowed to an unwilling walk. The descent was sharp. Soon Happy was dancing with the buggy, pausing at each step to hold it back. "Now if Katie were here, we'd have to get out and walk!" For Katie was cautious, timid of accidents. Anne kept her seat, jerking to and fro with the hold-back. They came waltzing down through the trees onto the flat, forked road and turned in a wide arc toward Winterfield Center. And there at the next bend, wobbling through a golden shower, came a young man on a bicycle.

Hastily, Anne tilted her hat and smoothed her skirt. "Whoa," she said to Happy, who stopped, grudgingly obedient, until the young man came abreast and stood down from his bicycle.

He touched his hat. Sun and shade speckled a thin, sharp face which the twins, in their last amicable chat, had agreed to call "handsome."

"Mornin'," he greeted her, and his eyes slid to her hair — "Anne."

"What would you do if I left my hair loose?"

"Oh, I think I'd know you. You have a different look." Anne blushed with pleasure. "Anne, can I ride with you?"

"But you're going the other way."

"Well. In fact, I was on my way to see you."

"To see me, or Katie? Or both of us?" Katie would have winced to hear.

But Ernest Fiske did not wince. He smiled; rested his bicycle against a stone wall, climbed in and reached for the reins.

"I'll drive, Ernest. Happy knows my handling. Tl-tl-tl."

Happy's ears shot forward. She had been resting resignedly, left hind foot propped lightly against right front foot; now she swished her tail, blew joyously (Ernest whipped out a handkerchief), and set off, clop-clop.

"Do you always go this fast?"

"I'm in a hurry. I'm going to Little's for sugar. Are you coming tonight?"

"I should say so! That's why I was comin' to see you."

"Should be fun. We planted a few red ears."

"Anne, listen. Slow down a bit."

Glancing sideways, Anne saw that Ernest was in earnest. Sweat stood on his moustache. "Oh, all right. Waaalk." Happy trotted determinedly a few more steps. *"Waaalk."* The buggy slowed to a mild amble. Happy's rump swayed gently now, and speckled shade and drifting leaves passed slowly over all.

Still, Ernest hesitated. He gnawed his lip, removed his hat, and twirled it on a finger; jammed it back on, and said, "You'll have to let me drive."

"What!"

"Confound it, I can't say this with you drivin'! Just ain't proper!"

"Well, if it means that much to you!" She handed him the reins. She was having trouble breathing, as though her ferris waist were tightening by itself. Hope struggled in her mind with sensible doubt.

"Spirited, ain't she!"

Ernest had a heavy hand on the reins. She would have to take them back, shortly.

"All right, Ernie, you're driving. Now, what is it?"

2

Once before this, Anne and Ernest had been alone together. That had been on the first day of school.

Later in the season, Anne would ride the school team with the children, especially on cold, wet days. But that first day of school she walked. She followed the gravity-flow trough up to the spring, and paused to drink from her hand where the water leaped, cold-bright, down the rocks. Then she took the hill path over the stile, through the pasture, past the sugarhouse. The milkers watched her come among them and barely made way for her, swishing tails and twitching ears, trotting aside at last with a gentle jiggling of udders. Goldenrod bowed and swayed in the morning breeze. The sky cleared bright, deep blue; and against this brightness shone a silver cocoon, a web of mist, clinging to a dewy milkweed.

Anne broke off that section of milkweed and carried it with her, peering through the web to glimpse the live shadow at its heart. Below, the train hooted; the Northampton Bullet rumbled past Winterfield, wending its way through the hill towns and beyond. She saw its smoke, black above the hill.

"Mornin', . . . Anne. What are you up to?"

In her surprise, Anne almost dropped the cocoon. She had thought she had the hillside to herself. And here in her path stood Ernest Fiske, dressed for work in overalls, checked shirt and unraveling straw hat, which he touched with a polite, ineffective gesture.

"My goodness! Ernie, what are *you* up to?"

"On my way to Graves' orchard."

"You'll be awfully late." The hill path was the longest way there.

"Well, I wanted to see you. Wish you a happy what-you-call-it — term."

"Thanks."

They stood in the path silent, embarrassed. A long moment dragged. Ernest waved at the cocoon. "What you want that for?"

"I'm taking it to school."

"I thought they did the three R's in school!"

"With me, they do four R's: reading, writing, 'rithmetic, rhyme. This is the rhyme."

"You mean, they get to write rhymes about it?"

"That's a good idea! I hadn't thought of it, yet."

He blurted, "I wish I was in your school! I mean, no I don't, because if I was in school we . . . What I mean . . ." He recovered himself. "What I wanted to ask you, are you going to the Grange social Saturday night?"

"I expect." She spoke coolly, offhand. It would never do to let Ernest guess the furor this same Grange social was stirring up at home! The mending, the washing, the search for the curling irons —

"Because if you are, I can drive over and pick you up. It's . . . on my way." Not exactly.

"Katie *will* be pleased! She hates my driving. And my folks are going to Aunt Alma's that night, instead."

"Well, then. Well, I guess I'd best get to work."

"I guess."

"See you Saturday night."

"We'll be looking for you."

He touched a finger to his dilapidated hat, and passed.

From the top of the hill path, Anne looked down on Winterfield Center and the small school beside the white-steepled church. Her pupils were gathering in the school yard. The little girls, primped and ironed and starched, were too conscious of their new school dresses to play, or even to sit on the outside bench. They stood about chatting, "for all the world like a Ladies' Benevolent Society!" The boys wrestled, climbed, hunted for snakes behind the backhouse. Charitably, one guessed that their hair had been brushed, combed, and slicked before they left home.

Anne almost forgot the surprising meeting with Ernest and its possible significance. Eagerly she hurried down the hill and passed through the gathering crowd, smiling her teacher-smile. She went in through the door that the children had not ventured to open.

Books, bell and rapper lay ready on her battered desk. Readers were stacked on the end of the first bench — no, they weren't. The readers were laid out along the table neatly, like dishes set for dinner.

Green light filtered through the leaves pressing the windows. In the water-green dimness, someone moved. A young girl stood up behind the table.

"Morning, Sallie." Anne smiled; not her teacher-smile; her glad-to-see-a-good-friend smile.

Sallie Flower, at fourteen, was the oldest girl in school. Anne had not expected to see her this year. The Flowers were not education crazy. It must have cost Sallie a struggle to wrest this last school year from housework, fieldwork and baby-sitting. As Sallie stood against the light Anne noticed that the summer had changed her. Last spring she had been a child, lanky and awkward. She was still awkward, but filled out. New breasts pulled her middy out of shape. She had

curled her hair — Anne could smell the singed ends
— and light-brown ringlets tossed and bounced on her
stooped shoulders. She's grown pretty, Anne thought,
surprised. Very pretty.

Aloud she said, "Sallie, find a glass or jar for this
cocoon? It can stand on my desk, like a flower."

"Pretty as." Sallie smiled. In her pale-blue eyes
Anne saw delight.

"I knew you'd like it!" She had been thinking of
Sallie, all along.

"Sallie Flower is special," she told Katie later, as
they met to press their skirts for the Grange social.
Katie stood the ironing board beside the range, and
pinned a scorched sheet around its fat padding. Anne
reached into the warming oven, fished out the handle,
and clamped it on the glowing flatiron.

"You first," Katie offered. "Mine will take ages."
For at this time the twins were yet friends. She filled
the sprinkling bottle from the pantry trough; then settled in the kitchen rocker to wait, her pink party skirt
draped over the arm.

"I don't know how you dare to wear pink, with your
hair. Our hair." Anne laid her own skirt on the
board; a sober blue, proclaiming "party" only by its
fancy buttons and ruffle. "What I mean about Sallie
Flower . . ." Warily she tested the iron against a damp
finger. "There. What I mean is, she loves things."

"You mean like apple pie and willow plate?"

"Don't tease!" Anne swept the iron up and down the
easy part. "I'm talking about Poetry."

"Oh. Poetry." From their childhood, "Poetry" was
their word for all that lay beyond rhyme, meter,
words. "Does she like Emily?"

"As much as we did!" Anne noticed a flash of surprise cross Katie's face. "But you know whom I like
now, Katie? Someone I've just discovered. Listen."
Bending to flute the ruffle, she recited warmly:

The Female equally with the Male I sing
Of Life immense in passion, pulse and power,
Cheerful, for freest action form'd under the laws
      divine,
The Modern Man I sing.

"It's certainly grand," Katie admitted doubtfully.

"I'm going to show Sallie that book!"

"Oh, no!" Katie started. The pink skirt slipped to the floor.

"Why ever not?"

"Well. Do you think it's really what Sallie needs?"

Fluting expertly, Anne mused. She thought of Sallie's flourishing curls, new breasts, grave eyes. "Yes, it's just what she needs; she has to raise her sights if she's not to turn all flighty and silly, like everybody else."

Rescuing her skirt from the clean floor, Katie raised indignant eyes. "No wonder the girls call you a snob!"

"They even called me a snob in normal school! Even Grandma used to twit me with it!" Anne sighed. "I rely on you to interpret me to a hostile world!"

"I haven't been doing very well, have I." At Katie's sad tone, Anne glanced up from the ruffle.

"Oh, I was joshing! I can take care of myself — there, I've scorched it!" She thumped the iron back on the range to reheat, and spread the next section of skirt on the board.

"That's what Grandma said," Katie agreed. " 'The world had better watch out for itself, with Annie in it!' "

For an instant, the bright, tidy kitchen dimmed. Anne still mourned their grandmother Catherine. Her southeast room upstairs was still hers; the bed was spread with her quilt, her workbasket stood on the dresser, and Aunt Nellie's wretched sampler hung beside the door. Passing that door, Anne could still feel a breath of Grandma's presence, like a lingering, fading echo.

"You were her favorite," Katie said softly.

"Maybe, in a way." Anne licked her finger, tested the iron. "Opposites attract, they say. You and she were really closer."

"In a way." Katie rocked happily in and out of a shaft of sunshine.

"You have the gift!" Anne suddenly saw it. "The lovecharm!"

"Oh! Do you mean that?"

The twins believed that certain people wore a love-charm, an invisible, magic jewel, whose wearer must inevitably be loved. Meeting such a favored person, one fell helplessly in love; one felt understood, valued, and relentlessly attracted. But such people were rare. Grandma was one; Uncle Myron was one; and there had been a teacher, in school.

Lifting the iron, Anne looked at Katie. Katie leaned forward, breathlessly awaiting her answer. Katie was pert and lovely, and young. This should be enough. But Anne could almost see the love-charm, like a locket at Katie's throat.

"Ayah. Grandma gave it to you."

Katie sighed, and rocked back. "Oh, I hope you're right! It's true, people like me. I've never had any trouble with people."

Anne nodded, a trifle grimly.

"But now, now it matters. You know what I mean, Annie?"

"Ah. Er." Anne thumped the iron.

"You know tonight, Ernie's picking us up?"

Thump.

"Annie. Do you think maybe Ernie likes me?"

"Can't help but like you." Especially if you have the love-charm. And yet . . .

Anne whisked her skirt off the board, Katie popped up and laid hers on. "Do you want my blue ribbon tonight?" she asked kindly. "I'm wearing the yellow."

"Yellow with *pink?*"

"I can get away with it."

"Pride goes before! I'll fetch the ribbons. We almost forgot to press them!" Anne swept out of the kitchen as Katie picked up the iron.

"Is this iron hot? Ouch!"

3

When Anne, Ernest and Katie entered the Grange Hall, the first dance was in progress.

> *Hurry hurry hurry let's go,*
> *Over and then below,*
> *And everybody swing your own —*

From the dais, Amos Flower called. His wife banged the piano, his brother fiddled. The rest of the Flower tribe was dancing, along with a scattering of Cooks, Stones and Littles. Children formed one whole square, young people another, and the third was a mixture of ages; and off to the side, behind the re-

freshment stand, a pair of laughing toddlers swung in
and out of lantern light.

So Anne was not surprised to see Sallie, hand in
hand with Otis, prance down the center, "over" one
couple and "below" the next, swing and promenade.
Otis was a good six years older than Sallie, and not
the soberest young man in town; but, Anne thought, it
was probably better than dancing with one's brother.

She sidled past the far-flung children's square and
sat down on the sidelines, smoothing her skirt and
settling her feet out of the way; for she expected to
sit there most of the evening. Katie rustled to sit down
by her, head turned the other way, toward Ernest.
With a final swing, flourish and thump the dance
ended, the squares broke up. Muttering to Katie, Ernest rose and rushed past, making for the refresh-
ment stand.

"Olive's here," Katie whispered, "with Guess Who."
Anne nodded. "Cyrus is looking at you." Momentarily, hope stirred Anne's heart. But Cyrus looked
away as a piano-rumble warned, "Form your squares."

The children came running back to their square.
The hall was filling, now there were five squares.
Ernest pushed past Anne and offered Katie a lemonade.
"Oh! Thanks!" Katie looked up, astonished. She ac-
cepted the drink unwillingly; and Ernest turned to
Anne.

Anne had always resented the male prerogative.
Rare was the Ladies' Dance, when giggling girls descended upon their chosen partners. If she could
have chosen here and there, Cyrus one time and
Sammy the next, she would have danced every dance
at every social. But that was not the way of it. Only
in case of an emergency — a girlfriend vanished into
the cloakroom, nobody to choose from but fat housewives — only then would a young man approach her.
It used to hurt; but now that the hurt was habitual,
she scarcely noticed. "It must be my hair," she
thought, taking the calloused hand that Ernest offered.

"He must think I'm Katie!" For tonight she had left her hair loose, swinging curly under the starched ribbon.

"Form your squares!" Amos bellowed. "One couple needed down front here!" Ernest pulled Anne along, zig-zagging among the squares to the empty spot Amos pointed out. They were head couple. Otis and Sallie were third. Sallie held her head high, in contrast to her meek school-day stance; her pretty, very young face was still flushed from the last dance. Otis held her hand casually. He stood loose, smiling about. (After the last social Mama had remarked on Otis's "roving eye.")

Mrs. Flower whacked the piano. The square grabbed hands and circled eight, twisting, pulling, blending rhythms. Before they returned to place they were caught up in a collective rhythm, safely beyond private awkwardness. Fat Mrs. Pease moved as lightly as Anne. Old Mr. Stone's stoop had vanished, his glance sparkled youthfully. Anne was conscious of Ernest's firm hand in hers, and the disturbing masculine smell of his plaid shirt. Beyond this was only lightness, a tide of music and motion.

The first two ladies cross over
And by the gentlemen stand —

She stepped smartly down the center, holding out a hand to Sallie, who touched and passed. Otis met her with an extra butterfly twist, which surprised her not at all because it blended with their collective rhythm, and because her heightened senses had guessed it coming. She saw Sallie standing now beside Ernest, a schoolgirl again, shy beside a grown man, poised to leave him. But not yet.

The two side ladies cross over
And all join hands —

Calm and smiling, the two plump housewives sashayed across the square, lifted on music into grace.

> *Honor to your corner,*
> *Honor to your own.*
> *Take your corner lady*
> *And promenade her home—*

Mr. Stone had an individual step, a kind of drawled
shuffle. Trying to match him, Anne was dragged back
to momentary self-consciousness; and so she happened to see Katie's face.

Katie sat demurely, watching Ernest across the circle. Astonished hurt showed in her eyes, but her lips
held a faint, superior smile. So often had Anne worn
exactly that smile, she understood it perfectly. And
she exulted.

Later, she thought she must have been completely
under the spell of the music; that relentless, joyful
music which to the dancer is the heartbeat of an up-
lifted soul and to the wallflower sounds like a funeral
march. The music invaded her, she forgot who she
was, where she was, with whom she swung, do-si-
doed, and promenaded. She knew only that she
moved lightly, breathlessly, with grace beyond her
own, and in step with all the others.

From the dais, Amos Flower wove the dance.
Cryptically he called steps and figures. His calls were
so well known that no one had to listen; and they
were often drowned out by claps and exultant thumps
and shouts. Yet he presided. His calls spun a web of
motion, joyous to perform, beautiful to watch — unless one sat unwillingly beside the wall.

The set rumbled to a crashing end. Mrs. Flower
lifted her hands dramatically from the piano, her
brother-in-law squeaked the fiddle and laid it aside.

> *Take her there, you know where,*
> *'Cause that's the end of the call!*

Slowly the reeling hall settled. Anne's vision cleared. A few feet away, Sallie hung on Otis's shoulder. Sallie was very young for Otis. Troubled, Anne threw a glance at the dais, where the elder Flowers were gulping lemonade. Mrs. Flower, leaning on the piano, watched Otis. Crafty calculation firmed her flabby face.

Anne danced every dance until ten-thirty, when the social broke up. Counting coup, she remembered dancing four sets with Ernest, two with Ansel, one with old Mr. Stone and one with her pupil Eban, Sallie's young brother. She thought that Ernest had also danced a good deal with Katie. Certainly, Katie did not sit out again!

"Between the two of us, we did all right," she told Mama on Monday. "We kept them busy."

"All of them? Or mostly Ernest?"

They were scalding tomatoes, skinning and squashing them into jars. Seeing Katie's eyes go hard, Anne tried to steer away from the subject of Ernest. "Mama, Sallie Flower danced with Otis all evening!"

"Well; her papa calls."

"And her mother plays. But they're not keeping an eye on her."

Mama shrugged. "You're not responsible, Annie, you're just the schoolteacher. I wouldn't worry. All the Flower girls commence young."

Katie unbent enough to giggle. "And when they come to get married, they don't fit the wedding dress! They ought to put a panel here, and leave it permanent." She passed her red-stained hands across her waist.

"Katie!" Mama looked reproach. "That's no way to talk about neighbors! At least the Flower girls do get married!"

"But" — Anne paused, squashing down tomatoes — "they marry so darn young! How can they be sure that's what they want?"

Mama went on dunking and peeling; but she looked a question across the table.

"I mean, well, Sallie's a bright girl. She might want something else."

"Like what?" Katie challenged.

"She might go to the City, for instance."

"And take dictation?" Katie's voice held incredulous scorn.

"There must be more than that to do in the City."

Mama chuckled. "I'm kind of glad I don't have your brains, Annie! Seems to me they make you a mint of trouble. You can always see a problem where nobody else sees one. Like the time you came home from school, you were nine or ten, you said, 'Mama! I don't believe Noah's dove made those tracks on the doorstone!' And you worried it, and you worried it, till you found out what did. Nobody else ever bothered!" She took up a fork and mashed down her jarful. "Now I hope you won't worry and worry about is it worth your while to marry!"

"Is there some hurry?" Anne smiled, but Katie pouted.

"Gather ye rosebuds while ye may." Mama nodded, and hummed the tune. Anne sang alto. But Katie worked on in silence, while sunshine touched the table and the tomato jars shone like jewels.

They stewed the leftover tomatoes for supper, with biscuits, cream gravy and pumpkin pie. Orin pushed his plate back at last, and accepted tea. "Going to have a visitor tonight."

"Who's coming, Papa?"

"Friends of yours, ayah."

"Did he say," Katie asked gently, *"who* he's coming to see?"

"No, ma'am, he did not. Just said he's thinking of paying a call at the Bennetts after supper. If I was you, I'd pop into my best bib and tucker."

"Excuse me . . ." Katie rose gracefully and made

for the back hall, pausing to remind Anne, "It's your night to do up, you know."

Sighing, Anne cleared the table and tied on her apron. Orin lingered in the dining room with tea and the *Gazette*. Mama leaned over the Rochester lamp. Upstairs, hasty steps told of Katie's excitement.

Thoughtfully, Anne poured hot water in the dishpan on the kitchen table. She had the dishes half done when the poem that had been churning around inside broke into words. She floundered with the dishes, snatching at the words drifting like milkweed seeds through her mind. She must get these words down quick in the secret journal, before she lost them —

Leaving the dishes in the pan she sped through the dining room toward the front stairs. Orin looked up inquiringly. "I'll be back in a jiffy — don't let Mama touch those dishes — " She flitted into the sitting room.

Ernest said loudly, "I don't know too much about poetry, but I like that."

Anne paused. Ernest must have arrived while she was doing up. And Katie had not called her! And where were they, anyhow? Would Katie dare open the sacred parlor doors for Ernest?

Katie replied, "She's very clever, you know. Not like me."

"I think you're remarkably clever!"

"Now, I don't want you to think I'm apologizing. I'm quite as clever as her, in my way. You should taste my apple pie! But I sure don't have her head for Poetry. Listen, here's another one."

"Wait a minute, Kate. Will she mind?"

"She's doing up, she'll be a while. Besides, it's all right if you *like* it. It's if you *didn't* like it she'd mind. Now listen." Katie lowered her voice to the solemn, rather mournful murmur she considered proper to Poetry.

Was this possible? Would Katie dare? Could she be so heartless? She could. Low but clear came the dreadful, secret words. In that respectful, remorseless tone Katie read:

> *"At morning mid the lilacs bright*
> *I sense a shadow, left from night.*
> *At dusk I wait, and linger late,*
> *To feel among the lilacs — Fate."*

Ernest mumbled.

"Ayah, it's a trifle vague. It's about a game we used to play when we were little."

"Nostalgia?"

"Exactly.

> *A sorrow haunts these lilac trees,*
> *A sorrow gentle as a breeze."*

Anne came in a rush to the front hallway. The parlor doors were folded shut. No light flickered through the crack.

"That's nice," Ernest decided.

"Oooo! Here's a *new* one I never saw before!"

The voices came in through the sitting-room window. So warm was the Indian-summer night, Katie was entertaining on the front porch. Through the window, Anne spied pale lantern-glow on the wide-open pages of her Very Secret Journal.

> *"Secretly forming,*
> *Suspended in mist,*
> *A chrysalis dreams of*
> *Fluttering wings,*
> *Sunshine and dew.*
> *It dreams, like you . . ."*

On each side of the wide front door Orin had placed heavy old settles; and over the whole latticed porch climbed a bittersweet Grandma Catherine had planted. Its heavy-clustered berries hung like grapes through the latticework. Katie and Ernest sat close together on one settle, not facing each other, as Anne had imagined, poring over the Very Secret Journal. Ernest looked up anxiously as Anne burst upon them.

"I hope you don't mind — "

Katie held onto the book and raised her voice. "It dreams, like you, a wide future of — "

Anne wrenched the book out of her hands. Much as she might have said, or choked, to Katie in private, before Ernest's guilty eyes she was speechless. Swallowing tears of fury, gripping the book to her heart, she rushed indoors and upstairs, to Grandma's room.

The door stood open. The room was dark, but not empty. A lingering reflection of comfort enfolded Anne. She plunked down on the bed, still clutching her desecrated secret. What would Grandma have said?

"There now. It ain't all that bad. They're *good* poems, after all."

"But how could she do it! How *could* she!" Anne wept, but very softly because the porch was right under Grandma's window.

"There's a saying, you know, 'All's fair in love and war.' Maybe Katie's in love."

"What's that got to do with it? She had no right!"

"Lucky you hadn't written a poem about Ernest!"

"Oh, my Godfrey!" If Katie had turned one page more she would have come upon a beginning: "When I (observe, behold) consider your hands with the dark hairs upon them" —

"Calamitous," Grandma agreed. "But it didn't happen."

"It didn't happen because I got there first! I don't see how she had the heart! What could she have done worse! By golly, I hope Katie *is* in love! Then I can get back at her, maybe!" Anne swallowed, calmed her breathing. The fire of grief in her froze abruptly into determination. She leaped up and marched out of Grandma's comforting room and down the hall to her own. She stowed the Very Secret Journal in a new place, under a pile of school papers; then she lit the lamp, and sat down before the mirror.

Quickly she tore the hairpins out of her bun. Bright hair spilled down her shoulders. Smiling ferociously, she noted the whiteness of her little, even teeth. Tear-slime shone on her cheeks, her eyes looked sick; but that was temporary. "I've got the brains," she said grimly, aloud, *"and* the looks. What has Katie got that I haven't?" Deep inside, an apologetic voice murmured, "The love-charm."

Somewhere under all this emotion there was a poem still bubbling about; the poem that had led to this terrible, fortunate discovery. Anne paused to examine it, and burst into bitter laughter.

It would have been a poem about Katie.

4

A week later Anne stood outside the old sugarhouse at the top of the pasture. It was a warm, bright afternoon; leaves rustled orange, the pasture tumbled golden down to the house, which sat in its walled yard like a red hen in a nest. Walking home over the hill path loaded down with books and papers, Anne paused outside the sugarhouse. She thought of its cool emptiness. In there, she could dump the books in the firebox and sit at the long table, rest her aching arms. She made for the door.

The sugarhouse was used only during the late winter, early spring; Anne thought she was the only person who ever stopped by here, and she had not turned into the maple grove for a week. Yet . . . the tall goldenrods before the door had been pushed aside, knocked over. A trodden path led through the weed-jungle to the rough door.

Suddenly anxious, Anne glanced about. Here, where she had thought to be alone, someone had recently come. Someone might still be here, watching from hiding! Goodness, suppose she had muttered to herself, as she did — very occasionally — on this solitary walk; suppose she had scratched herself, thinking no one saw! Nervously watching the door behind the trampled goldenrod, she patted her bun smooth.

Behind the door — a giggle; and a whisper.

Anne clutched her books close, glanced about rather wildly. "Funny *I* should hide," flashed through her mind. "It's *our* sugarhouse, after all! That's a trespasser in there!" But she darted forward through the weeds and flattened herself against the wall, behind the door.

That giggle and whisper had sounded somehow nefarious; conspiratorial; it was also familiar. Anne might giggle like that in her sleep, wandering in vaguely guilty dreams.

Something slithered on the far side of the wall. A male voice murmured. A female voice cooed. And Anne recognized it.

Fury was her first reaction. She would have rushed into the sugarhouse waving a witch's wand of school papers, but that the wave of fury was followed instantly by a wave of embarrassment. Lord knew what she might see on the other side of that thin wall! What

hideous revelation, what intimacy unthinkably vio-
lated! But the fury remained, steaming in her like sap
in a shallow pan. "And to use our sugarhouse! Without
a by-your-leave, just to walk up here and close the
door and . . . all day!" Anne felt personally injured, as
though something had been stolen from her. Examining
the feeling, she recognized its folly. "Nothing to do with
me. I'm not responsible, I'm just the schoolteacher."
And then came the third wave: sorrow.

> Secretly forming,
> Suspended in mist,
> A chrysalis dreams
> Of fluttering wings,
> Of sunshine and dew.
> It dreams, like you,
> A wide future of
> Wonderful things . . .

which would never now take place. The cocoon had
been ripped from the stalk, the silk torn and scattered.
"All the Flower girls commence young." And once
commenced, they went on and on. They married, bore
baby after baby, washed, cooked, helped in the fields;
they were gap-toothed crones at forty.

"It's not *fair*," Anne had complained to Mama when
the Facts of Life became more or less clear to her.

"Hush shush! It's the way the Lord planned it."

Anne had continued to think it rotten planning.
Now she leaned against the sugarhouse and listened to
the rustle and creak of Sallie's ruin, and wished she
knew some good, round, powerful bad words. It was
so darn unfair! Otis would presently emerge, pleased
and proud, with his future perfectly intact; unless Sallie
could snare him for good.

She was still fighting herself, vainly trying to still the
tumult of confused, outraged, sympathy, when without
warning the door swung and banged against her side.

She flattened thinner; and Otis swaggered past, just as she had imagined — except that he had red hair.

"You didn't fergit anything?" Sallie hovered in the doorway. Through the crack, Anne glimpsed blue gingham. Sallie sounded confident, complacent, quite unconscious of her ruin. Anne wanted to grab and shake.

"Nope; but you did." Departing, Otis glanced back; he was Hayden Taylor. "You left that grammar in the firebox."

He sashayed off, pushing through the weeds; and Anne heard him whistling down the hill path. Muttering, Sallie withdrew from the doorway. Her footfalls crossed the floor to the firebox and returned; she stepped out into sunshine, smoothing her bouncing brown curls, the grammar cradled lovingly in one arm. Like an innocent schoolgirl whose life opens before her, a rich valley crossed by forking roads; seeming almost as contented and carefree as such a girl, Sallie Flower wandered away, cuddling her grammar. "You poor fool," Anne thought violently. "You might as well have left it! You won't need it!" Then she fell to reflecting on the unexpected transformation of Otis Graves into Hayden Taylor.

Anne closed the door. Slowly she regained the path. Slowly she descended the home fields, still reflecting. In the midst of gloomy conclusions she heard the lonely wail of the Northampton Bullet from the next valley. The train was puffing along the valley floor — she saw its plume of black smoke — through the golden hill towns, and beyond.

5

Anne went to war with Katie. After school hours she became a new person, a completely different young woman. She left her hair loose, topped with a jaunty ribbon. She smiled till her mouth ached, and deliberately sparkled her eyes.

Nothing was said. Anne and Katie were not speaking. Mama ventured to remark, but Anne saw her sidelong glances. The hired men greeted Anne more cheerfully, she noted. And Sunday after church the gossiping neighbors seemed uneasy when she stepped into their midst. Unsure which twin she was, they did not want to ask! To be safe, they called her "Miss Bennett." Anne laughed inside herself, a cold, lonesome laugh.

Katie pouted. She tried to fight back. "You're not flouncing about here in your best skirt on a Monday!" Mama scolded her. "I thought you were grown up!" Katie bought new ribbons and polished her boots. She sparkled no less than Anne, but she could no longer eclipse her. Orin beamed proudly upon his pair of twins. "I never saw them so bright!" He remarked to Mama. Anne heard Mama snort.

Anne went to war, and she employed the necessary weapons. But deep inside, her heart shuddered. Every school morning, facing Sallie across the battered table, she remembered and wondered. "It's only for now," she consoled herself. "I don't have to *be* a Sallie, just *seem like one;* for now." But then, wasn't she deceiving Ernest?

The morning of the husking bee she pinned her hair back and let her face assume its natural, grave expression. This was a busy morning. She hung lanterns. She meant to clean the dining room and tidy it for refreshments. But then Mama said, "Annie, would you drive down to Little's for me?" Anne still thought that evening would be time enough for smiles and sparkles and ribbons; she took off in a rush, rattling down the rough road in a shower of golden leaves, never thinking to primp or fuss; she did not expect to meet Ernest on the road to Winterfield.

He caught her undisguised, disarmed, jolted and disheveled, flushed with speed, and autumn air. Even so, Ernest fumbled for words. He twirled his hat upon his finger, and blurted at last, "You'll have to let me drive."

"What!"

"Confound it, I can't say this with you drivin'! Just ain't proper!"

Anne had trouble breathing. Her ferris waist seemed to tighten by itself, she could feel her cheeks turning pink. She could hardly believe her victory. Was this really all she needed to do — smile, gleam, tie on a bright ribbon?

"Well, if it means that much to you." She handed Ernest the reins.

"Spirited, ain't she!"

"All right, Ernie, you're driving. Now, what is it?"

"What I wanted to say, Annie — what, what do you want to do with yourself?"

Cautiously she watched him from under her hat brim. "How much choice do you think I have?"

"More than most girls. For instance, my sisters want to get married."

"Perfectly natural."

"Ayah, so it is. But do you . . . want to get married?"

"Ah. That would depend."

"As I thought! You have plans, haven't you."

"I have some ideas." She thought of the letter she had left in the mailbox, under the up-thrust red flag.

"I sort of guessed that, after that night we . . . we looked at your poetry. Remember?"

"Oh yes."

"Well, I thought to myself, a girl like that, she can do something better for herself than putter around a farm kitchen."

"I think that's a darn good thing to do!" Indignantly, Anne came to Mama's rescue, and Grandma's; and was disconcerted when Ernest turned a brightening eye upon her.

"Do you really? Cannin' and cookin' and gardenin' and washing' and youngsters? When maybe you could be writin', say, advertisements instead?"

"How on earth did you know I had thought of that?"

"I've thought of it myself."

"You!"

"Sure. I used to make up poems too; not such good ones though."

"You did!"

"One time I did one about autumn leaves, like now." With one hand Ernest caught a passing maple leaf. Gripping it in tense fingers he looked down at it as he said, "You know the story Miss Graves read us about the girl with the shower of gold? What's her name, Dana. About that."

Anne gasped. Ernest blushed. "I always think of that when the leaves fall, like now. Us poets are loony, you know." He dropped the leaf over the side and faced Anne. "Well. Do you want to get married?"

Anne sighed. She had just discovered a real friend in Ernest. But several voices murmured from the back of her mind.

"Fact is, Ernie, I'm discombobulated."

"You haven't decided?"

Winterfield Center joggled into view, chastely white amid tawny fields.

"I haven't decided anything."

"Will you decide pretty soon?"

"I'll put my magnificent mind right to it."

"See you tonight." He handed back the reins.

"Your bicycle — "

"Ain't far back." Ernest touched finger to hat and swung lightly down. Feeling the subtracted weight, Happy swished her tail and broke into a trot. Winterfield Center bobbed close. Anne looked back to wave goodbye, but Ernest was already around the bend.

❧ 6 ❧

Shortly after supper the guests commenced to arrive. Anne was lighting the Rochester lamp on the dining-room table when the first wheels crunched up past the bow window. "Someone's here!" she called to whoever was moving about in the kitchen.

A strained silence followed. It was Katie, then, unwilling to answer her. After a long moment came Katie's reluctant voice. "Nobody."

Mama came bustling down the backstairs and through the hall, her fresh dress crackling starch, plump hands patting her bun smooth. "Nobody but your uncle Myron!" she clucked, and scurried to the door. Calls and laughter resounded from the barnyard.

"Katie," Anne called, trying hard to sound friendly, "put the doughnuts to warm." She slipped out of her apron, hung it behind the door, smoothed her dress.

The Rochester's warm light washed an alarmingly perfect dining room, which Katie had spent half a day polishing. Willow plate gleamed; geraniums glowed on the window seat. Crossing to close the tasseled muslin

169

curtains, Anne saw lights approaching, bobbing up Bennett Road. "More coming! Warm the pies, too, Katie!" She gave the room a last, swift inspection. Here the guests would assemble for refreshments after husking. They would find a warm room, glowing pleasant gentility. "Looks like half the town's coming, Katie! Get out the big coffeepot!"

In wagons and buggies and on foot, the young people of Winterfield converged on the Bennett place. Within minutes the barnyard was crowded with horses, young men, girls, a few older people. Aunt Alma watched from the doorstone with bright, eager eyes. Uncle Myron led the assembly toward the barn, where Orin and Cyrus Little were lighting lanterns.

Olive Peters was there, and Ansel Cook; Otis Graves, with little Sallie Flower (Anne scowled fiercely); Hayden Taylor, Rowena Stone, Stacey Knight, Sammy Pease. And that last buggy lantern jogging up the road — that must be Ernest.

He came alone, of course. The whole town knew that Ernest Fiske was after one of the Bennett sisters; Anne suspected they were laying bets on which one. Her ferris waist tightened as she watched Ernie drive up. "I'm blushing!" she realized, and thanked the Lord for kind darkness. After their buggy ride this morning, it was difficult for her to look Ernest in the face.

She had given considerable thought to the matter he had raised; indeed, she had pondered it all day. And she had come to one conclusion, at least: "I do not love Ernie Fiske." Leastwise, not in the sense of "How do I love thee let me count the ways.'" The question remained, was that sort of love really necessary? Mama and Papa were happy together. Between them they had built a life as solid and sound as the old house, using hard work and good temper, and nary a trace of romance as far as Anne could see. It was that kind of life that Ernie wanted, and deserved. But did she?

Laughing, chatting, delightful suspense high in their voices, the crowd surged into the barn and around the enormous corn stack. Orin had set out three cider jugs. Ansel was already sampling one.

"How many red ears, Mr. Bennett?"

"One for each of you. But they're all on the bottom."

"Pass the jug clockwise — "

"Only after red ears — "

"Oh come on, one to get ready — "

Ernest came between the twins. To the ill-concealed amusement of all, Anne and Katie separated, and sat on opposite sides of the pile; leaving Ernest between Sallie and Rowena.

Tensely, the group sat looking at the pile. Girls tittered, young men shoved. Then Uncle Myron waddled into the circle of light, stooped and grabbed an ear. "Here goes! Ready, girls?" He stripped the ear — a plain yellow one — made a disgusted face, and tossed the ear into the basket behind him. "Come on! You fellows lazy or shy?"

"Let's go!"

"Eight hands around!"

The crowd tore into the pile. Husks flew, ears popped into baskets. "Yellow . . . yellow . . . yellow . . . I bet you didn't plant no red, Mr. Bennett!" Grabbing, husking, the crowd raised heat. Faces flushed. Back in the cool shadow Uncle Myron, Aunt Alma, Mama and Orin stood like wall-flowers at a dance, watching the excitement.

Anne glanced across at Ernest. His eyes were upon her. Her embarrassed gaze slid quickly aside, to Sallie.

Sallie's neck was flushed right down into the collar. Grabbing and husking with the rest, she laughed a shallow, strange laugh. Her eyes glinted weirdly. "I wish I didn't know!" Anne thought sadly. "Or I wish I could forget!"

"Oho!"

"Pay dirt!"

"Eureka!"

Otis held up a red ear. Girls gasped and laughed. Tension-lightning ran around the circle. "Well, how do you like that little beauty?" He waved the ear. "Now, let me see . . ."

Rising, he stalked around the circle, leering, holding the red ear like a candle. Rowena giggled and leaned away; Stacey hid behind Hayden; Olive put her hands over her eyes. Anne never moved. Like the young men, she watched Otis, amused. The notion that he might want to kiss her hardly crossed her mind.

He came very close, waving the ear and grinning. His breath soured hers. Abruptly, he lunged past her and rushed for Katie, who leaped up and skipped out of range. Slowly now, Otis sashayed on around the circle, then jumped at Sallie. Sallie hopped up, squawking. Ernest leaned back, slowing her retreat; and amid clucks and laughter Otis grabbed her, and planted a wet kiss on her cheek.

After this the work went more rapidly; a few moments later Anne saw her dread realized; Ernest knelt up, waving a red ear.

Katie went pale. Her fingers strayed absently through her hair as she stared at Ernest's find. "She cares," Anne thought. "Maybe she's in love, for what that's worth.'" She looked quickly back to Ernest.

The young men called encouragement, the girls enticed; they knew they were safe, he was after one of the twins. Ernest started around the circle toward Anne. His feet seemed to drag. Surely it could not take him this long to pass Rowena and Olive, even with appropriate threatening gestures!

"This one here's Anne," Hayden pointed out helpfully. "Katie's t'other one."

"I know," Ernest assured him. He sidled up to Anne, stooped, and looked almost seriously into her eyes.

She had given Ernest no answer, this morning in

the buggy. She had not known the answer. But at the bee, as she looked up into Ernest's half-grave eyes, the answer flooded hers. In the midst of the crowd, under the waiting gaze of Mama and Aunt Alma, Uncle Myron and all her friends, her eyes told Ernest the truth. She was no Sallie Flower. She was a modern young woman, aware of her possibilities, who had sent a letter; and who loved her sister more than she had ever thought of loving Ernest Fiske.

Ernest leaned closer. Male voices called encouragement. Anne watched his eyes harden and brighten, and the look of determined fun overspread his face, like sunshine when a thunderhead passes. He drew back, sidestepped, and swaggered past.

"Two bits!" Hayden shouted. "Bets are called!"

Stacey shoved a basket to trip Ernest. He hopped the basket, and proceeded to Katie. Katie did not leap up and run. She sat like a rag doll, one hand in her hair, the other gripping a half-husked corn ear. Embarrassed for her, Anne thought she looked up at Ernest like a soft-eyed calf.

And in the presence of hooting witnesses, to the clink of coins piling in Hayden's hands, Ernest knelt down by Katie and took her in his arms.

7

After church two Sundays later, Mama bustled about the kitchen making gravy. Anne set the table for the usual Sunday chicken feast; and then stole out to the porch.

Katie sat small in the corner of the right-hand settle. She looked very young for a woman about to marry. She twirled a ringlet absently about her forefinger, and stared mistily at the last of the golden shower rattling down from the yard maple. All around the maple, the yard was ankle-deep in yellow-brown leaves, crackly like paper. Through the near-naked branches the last brilliant sky of the season shone like summer. A gold and brown chipmunk darted smoothly in and out of the stone wall along the yard.

Anne sat down by Katie, and looked with her at the last of autumn.

Katie's voice was as soft as leaf falling upon leaf. "Annie. I'm sorry. I thought you didn't care like I did."

"You were right." Anne laid a hand over Katie's.

"And you know" — half laughing — "it wasn't

very bright of me, either. Turns out, he likes poetry!"

"I know."

"I thought he'd . . . Annie, I'm so sorry, I thought he'd bust his buttons laughing."

"All's Well That Ends Well."

A noise, vaguely musical, swelled indoors. Orin was experimenting with the new parlor organ. The rich smell of chicken floated out with the noise. Anne sighed, happily.

Katie whispered, "But it didn't end well for you."

"Oh, I think it did. I sent a letter."

"Letter to who?"

"After I found out about Sallie." Anne paused. The hand under hers moved inquiringly.

"I found out Sallie's not . . . really nice."

"You didn't know that?"

"Heavens! Did you?"

"The whole town knows. You ought to listen more to gossip!"

"And yet you didn't mind having her at the bee?" Anne asked thoughtfully.

"Well. I did mention it to Mama. She said it was none of our beeswax."

"She was right!"

"And she said Sallie will probably get married soon, anyhow."

"Yes, that's what I found out. And then I took to thinking harder about marriage, about the whole thing. And then the train went by."

"I don't follow."

"The Northampton Bullet. And I came home and wrote a letter to Mount Holyoke."

"The Female Seminary?"

"The College." Anne said it reverently.

"Annie! Might you go there?"

"Depends on what they say." But Anne's voice betrayed cautious confidence.

"And then, what?"

"Then the road will fork again."

"That's what you want?"

"Katie, I want to flutter like a butterfly in a meadow! I want to taste all the flowers!"

"That would sound good in a poem."

"It will. My next poem will be about you, and Mama and Papa — about home; how home is a cocoon."

"I'm not a poet. Explain?"

"Home is a beautiful, strong, silver cocoon. But the time comes to creep out, and fly."

"And never come back?" For the first time since she sat down, Anne looked at Katie. Tears were sliding down Katie's cheeks.

"Oh, it's just a poem, Katie! Of course I'll come back! You know . . ." Anne stared absently at the chipmunk, which had darted under the bare lilacs, and now sat on a micasparkled stone, washing its face like a cat. "You know, I think I really decided this years ago, when we were little, and we played that game — Glorinda — in the lilacs."

"Glorinda was no game!"

"I wasn't sure if you knew that. Did you really see her, it, too?"

"She wore a white apron. And so sad . . ."

"Well, you see" — Anne raised her voice, to be heard over the thunderous wheezings from the parlor — "I decided I wasn't going to be sad like that. I wasn't going to hang around waiting — "

"Waiting, yes, that's what she seemed — "

"Waiting for what? For Life to come and pull her up on a white horse and ride off with her? You can't wait for that, not these days!"

For these were the bright days of a new season, an adventurous, invigorating season, luminous as autumn. The dark evils of history were over and done. Slavery, savagery, bigotry, possibly War itself, were relegated to the Past. Women were slipping out of aprons, stepping out beyond the dooryard. The White Man had shouldered his burden all around the world, and Western Civilization, Christianity-based, Science-enriched, promised a New Age. The twins seemed to watch the chipmunk under the lilacs; but their minds saw the future, radiant and wide as the autumn sky beyond the branches.

The chipmunk noticed them, from the corner of its soft, dark eye; abruptly, it dodged out of sight.

"I don't know, Annie. Maybe I envy you."

"I may end up envying you! We'll have to wait and see how the story progresses. Papa isn't aiming to play at your wedding, I hope?"

Katie laughed. "Good Godfrey, no! Aunt Alma's dying to play. She's been practicing Lohengrin all week!"

From the top of the stairs they heard the first stammering of the wedding march. Anne drew a deep breath and held it, to keep back sudden, surprising tears.

The music fell upon expectant silence, like rain upon waiting earth. Down in the front hall, pale in the golden lamplight, faces crowded like flowers. Quietly eager, they all looked up the stairs at the wedding party. Uncle Myron leaned against the banister. Rowena and Olive and Stacey, Otis and Hayden and Sammy, Cyrus and Sallie and little Eban, crowded the hallway and the parlor door, which was wreathed in bittersweet. From th parlor came the whisperings and stirrings of most of Winterfield: Cooks and Littles and Stones, Fiskes and Bennett cousins, Peterses, Flowers, a representative Winter, and Reverend Jones. Under Aunt Alma's nervous fingers the parlor organ sang; and as its voice strengthened, the magic happened, as in a dance; this was no longer Aunt Alma's anxious fingering; this was music.

Elated, Aunt Alma pumped louder. The march called, invited, insisted. Orin pushed gently through to the foot of the stairs, looked up and grinned. He raised a hand to beckon the wedding party down; and Anne noticed how strange his hairy wrist looked, rising out of the immaculate cuff. Everything looked strange.

She stood with Ansel on the third step down, burdened with bittersweet. Her blue dress fairly crackled starch, her petticoats scratched viciously, and the ferris waist constricted her breathing. Or was it her heart, pumping like Aunt Alma on the organ, that nearly choked her? Against Mama's wishes, she had drawn her hair back into its usual, school-teacher bun, only pinning a butterfly ribbon on top to satisfy the occasion. She had explained, "I don't want to be mistaken for the bride."

But there was little danger of that. Katie, standing with Ernest on the top step, wore Grandma's white wedding dress. (It had needed extensive taking-in; Grandma Catherine, it seemed, had never been slender.) She carried more bittersweet; and her ringlets flourished, bouncing and shining and twining to her wast. Anne turned to look up at her, in that last moment as Orin beckoned.

Katie was looking at Ernest. She slipped her hand through his elbow; and Ernest smiled. He was no typical bridegroom, Anne saw with approval. More relaxed than any of them, he did not seem to mind who knew he was happy. He smiled around blandly at his bride, at Anne, down at Orin; he punched the best man's shoulder; and Ansel whispered to Anne, "Let's go; over and then below."

Anne plucked her skirt clear of the steps; ceremoniously, they descended toward the flower bed of faces.

In all the faces Anne recognized friendship, well-wishing, love. And like Aunt Alma — now playing like Wagner himself — she relaxed and expanded. The breath she had held exhaled; and the paper in her pocket crackled. Then she remembered that Orin had handed her a letter, and she had been too busy tacking Katie's loose hem to look at it. She had glanced without comprehension at the return address, then stuffed it into her pocket. But now, as she paraded down the stairs, that address flashed across her mind: Mount Holyoke College, South Hadley.

Moving down toward Orin she gave him a smile that perhaps looked like love and conspiratorial joy; but which was, in fact, inward-turned. At that moment she was not thinking of the marriage taking place of her sister's new life, or her parents' new life; but of her own.

She saw herself as a butterfly, dangling from the last silk thread of its torn cocoon. Deliberately, luxuriously, it spread new wings to dry in the sun. Within the hour it would wing away.

The Summer Palace 1950

Is this trip really necessary?
—*Anonymous*

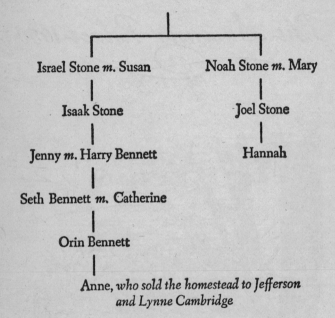

Israel Stone *m.* Susan

Isaak Stone

Jenny *m.* Harry Bennett

Seth Bennett *m.* Catherine

Orin Bennett

Anne, *who sold the homestead to Jefferson
and Lynne Cambridge*

Noah Stone *m.* Mary

Joel Stone

Hannah

1

Drifting up out of sleep, sun on closed eyes; darkness behind, below; what darkness, what light? And who am I?

A mushrooming darkness it was, a cloud of immense and final destruction. There would be fire beneath, but I saw no flame through the swirling mushroom of dark. There must have been pain, terror, shock; and millions of those moments too awful to bear, one moment for each person.

But I came drifting up safe. I knew to myself, "I am asleep, I have been dreaming. Actually, I am perfectly safe in a soft bed; and that light out there is calm sunlight." Actually, I am nesting like a fledgling bird in the highest, safest tree in the forest.

But wait a moment; let the fluttering eyelids lie; remember. There was more to that dream, gratefully behind me and sinking fast; there was a goodness in it, too. Under the mushroom-terror there was light, enclosed as in a seed. That was it! A seed of light waited to unfold. And if I lie still now, half asleep, I can just feel it unfolding, stretching tentative tentacles of light.

I know that feeling.

I know who I am, and why I cannot lie here any

longer. I am Lynne Cambridge, Mrs. Jefferson Cambridge, your wife, and we have two small kids.

Days later — maybe a week later, I lose track of time — the seed shot up, vigorous, from its compost of nightmare-reality. The kids were playing in the lilac hedge. From the temporary safety of the living room I heard their plaints, whines and shrieks. After each outcry — "You pig!" "Damn you!" — the breeze seemed to drop, birds hushed, as if listening. The very sunshine seemed to shrink and pale. After a moment nature came back to life. Robins twittered in the yard maple, a cool wind ruffled the lilacs — until the next screech. And then again the world hesitated, looking about itself, astonished.

After one particularly raucous scream I got up and looked out the window. I didn't want to open the window for fear of attracting attention. For almost half an hour, neither kid had yelled "Mommie!" It might even be they didn't know I was here!

Through the wavery glass the outside world rippled like an underwater scene. The cool green of leaves and grass undulated softly, sun-shot, shadow-dappled. Under the window the bank fell steeply to the lilac thicket and the stone wall edging the dirt road. Something white waved and twitched among the lilacs.

"You don't scare me, yah yah!" Chris yelled, "That's no ghost, it's you!"

That red splotch in the shadow was Chris's T-shirt. Copper hair curled above it. Allowing for the rippling effects, I was seeing Chris quite clearly. His hair flamed like a halo; one jeans leg was rolled up and the other had flopped down. In one infantile fist he held aloft the "ancestral" powder horn, properly a museum piece. "This'll bop you," he menaced. "This'll bop you good!"

I almost opened the window. Noah Stone His Horne was probably worth money. It was definitely not a toy. While I hesitated, Gwen pushed out of the bushes. Around her diminutive waist she wore your mother's damask tablecloth, that snowy fall of elegance, fussily embroidered, truly ancestral. "I wasn't *trying* to scare you," she retorted angrily, "I was looking for Emily May!"

I couldn't open the window. Half an hour of peace — a taste of blood! For another such half hour I would sacrifice more than a couple of antiques! Gingerly, gently, so as not to catch their quick eyes, I withdrew into the shadowed room.

On the old secretary lay a piece of blank paper. In this paper, clean and empty as a peaceful heart, I was about to draw.

At first I doodled. While I waited for an uprush of the inspiration I could feel seething inside like a geyser, I doodled maple leaves, dandelions, a stone wall. I tucked ferns in the crannies of the wall, and shaded it. Outside, an unusual silence fell. I glanced out.

Chris was writhing on the bank, seeking the best posture for perusal of a picture book. Chin in hands, wiggling, he stretched on his stomach. I could see the pages darkening with dirty thumb prints. Craning my neck, I squinted at its colors. If it was a book of my own illustrating — but no! I had never conceived those crude, primary splashes! It could go the way of Noah's horn and the tablecloth.

Gwen had vanished. I imagined her hunting snakes, or crouched on the back doorstone, filling in the fossil footprints with crayon; or swinging on the inner tube in the barn, momentarily dreamy. At five, Gwen was self-reliant. And there was little real trouble she could get into. I had removed the only real danger.

I turned back to my paper, pen in hand. I jumped when an eerie moan rose from across the hall. The moan gasped, broke off, resumed an octave higher; a macabre, off-pitch, one-finger rendition of Wagner's wedding march. I had found Gwen. The old parlor organ would hold her enthralled for another half hour.

I sketched a rectangle, filled in darks and halftones, tore it up. Six sheets later, I had totally forgotten kids, unwashed dishes, unmade beds, unplanned meals, dust under chairs. I no longer heard the Wagnerian wheeze from the parlor; even the old house no longer murmured continuously in my subconscious ear. The excitement that had been seething down under erupted. Light burst, mystery wrenched. A grandeur, just beyond, was stepping into light.

As desire rises unexpected, stirred by a gesture, a glimpse, so this deeper instinct in me responds to line, mass, color. And with the same uneasy, guilty delight, I surrender.

I no longer sat at the old secretary. I seemed to stand on the lawn, looking toward the immense, ancient maple whose branches roofed the rooftree. The scene opened like a flower; not so much a memory, as a vision. Rooted under the soil, under the house, its taproot surely touching earth's center, the maple soared to the sun. At its foot stood the old lady, craggy and rugged, sooner mortal than the tree, but no less serene. She lifted a peaceable face into sunlight. She planted her feet wide under the hem of her dowdy, long dress; her worn hands rested, clasped at her waist. With grave acceptance she contemplated a long past, a short, difficult future.

So she had stood, the day she came out from Boston for the closing. Gently, she insisted on showing us over the place herself, as though we had not inspected it with the agent (and sneaked a private viewing, besides). "The front half was built around 1830," she told us. "The barn, sometime later. The back ell is Colonial." She pointed out treasures for our appreciation: the bank where snowdrops would bloom between spring storms; the richest garden plot. "And your water. Gravity flow. Never freezes, never dries up."

You smiled and nodded. You bent toward her, touched her mottled hand. Impatiently, I wondered what she thought of us. Did she expect us to be here in March, when snowdrops bloom? Did she see me grubbing in the vegetable patch she showed us? I knew what I thought of *her;* slow, grave and kindly, she was a richly cultivated lady, product of a fast-dying culture. I heard my grandmother's voice in hers. I swallowed impatience, slowed my step, smiled when she turned to me. "When you have children," she said, "you can hang a swing from this maple. My twin sister and I used to swing here." And she patted the rough bark and glanced up, smiling, into the whispering leaves.

It took me a moment to recover. A wealthy Boston lady, yes; but also a country child, swinging in the maple-shade, probably barefoot. This piece never quite fitted into the puzzle. I was not about to *ask* her, and so invite reminiscences, a return to the kitchen, another cup of tea! (I was a little sorry later, when we happened upon her in *Who's Who.*)

But she was so slow, you remember, so maddeningly deliberate! And petty; emotionally involved. In the front bedroom that later became ours she lifted a child's sampler from the wall and carried it off. Not that it mattered; that sampler was no museum piece; but it annoyed me. And her presence in the house left an imprint. For a long time after, I could hear that bland old lady gently explaining, exclaiming. "Don't you think a sprig of bittersweet would be the thing for the front hall table?" Not a thing that would naturally occur to me! But, by heaven, I found myself out on the front porch, climbing on one of the seats to cut down a sprig!

In any case, there was no need for this guided tour. We had seen the house, inside and out, by ourselves. That's what I kept telling myself; you fell in love with it yourself. Later on, your pal Neal may have sealed the affair with his gratuitous approval; but that first hot, summer day, as we wandered up the dirt road we were hand in hand alone together. It was *we;* you and I, Jeff and Lynne.

We were out for a breather. The Bomb-haunted streets, the stifling apartment had grown too much for us. We were making money then, both of us. You had come far in the Agency, with you pushing me I was doing a book a season, we should have felt secure. But who could feel secure, with Russia shaking its fists? The End of the World loomed in daily headlines.

Out of breath from the long climb, we came out on the plateau. I said, "I don't think it leads anywhere, after all." I saw nothing ahead but sun-glinted woods; light slanting through the huge maples and across the dirt road; and a welcome stone wall to sit on.

But you said, "Lilacs! There'll be a cellar hole, come see!" You dragged me those last, reluctant steps to peer through the lilacs.

The bank rose to the roots of the shining maple; to the broken steps of a front porch; to the chipped and peeling housefront, with broken windows and sagging rooftree.

Ferns and weeds and drooping maple branches raggedly framed the house. Cool shadows swept the dooryard, as though the place were magically sealed from the rest of the hot, silent woods. Here birds sang, leaves rustled. Even the mica glowing in the stone walls gleamed coldly, like diamonds.

Your hand tightened on mine. We gaped, and watched. The house was obviously long deserted, yet we did not feel alone. I don't know how long we watched before pushing furtively through the thicket and up the bank.

First we climbed the porch steps. Gingerly, we sat on the seats, one on each side of the door. The bittersweet vine dangled, reaching for our hair. Shadow dappled the front door, with its wooden hinges and iron latch. Behind the door, silence listened.

We did not go in, then. We sat, absorbing it. I watched your face. I saw how tension softened, and melted, and you opened yourself to the spirit breathing around us. No stranger, seeing you at that moment, would have taken you for a highly successful illustrators' agent. You looked like a tired, rather dissipated child. I think you decided, then. Did you say to yourself, "In this place, we will make it?" Or did you say, "I can make it here. Lynne can help." I would like to know, although it doesn't matter now.

After a while you stood up. I stood with you. Slowly you wandered down the steps, through the long grass and weeds, around the side of the house. I followed, watchful for snakes. The house had once been red, but what was left of the weathered paint was faded pink. For the most part the boards were gray, crumbling at the knotholes. You stopped short at the back corner.

"I thought so!" you said, and pointed. I came up and looked over your shoulder. And there was an ell, like a second house, stretching away behind. It was more open here, away from the maple-shade. Sunshine drenched the bowed roof, with its missing shingles; and the knee-high golden grass, rippled by windsnakes.

"A big house." You tilted your head, tossed a wing of hair back from your forehead. "Built for a big family. A way of life . . ."

"You sound homesick!" I laughed, because nothing could be more alien to us than that way of life.

But you said, "I am homesick."

We waded through grass, cutting the corner to the back door. It was the same broad, firm sort of door, iron-latched. You stepped up on the high doorstone and pushed weeds away with your foot. You uncovered more and more doorstone, and pushed more, and found yet more stone. "Christ, it's endless! It's bedrock! Hey!" Down you went on your knees, nose to stone. Your finger traced through moss-crumbs, leaf mold. "Fossils!"

They were. In some unimagined time, tiny three-toed feet had run across a mud flat. "Before the hills were here," you breathed. I thought only a fantastic cataclysm could have preserved these irregular, irrelevant prints for us to wonder at.

Sitting back on your heels, you looked at me. "This place is magic."

I nodded.

"For us, just sunshine and grass would be enough. And no Bomb." You got up and brushed your seersucker knees. "Let's go down to the village. Inquire."

I hesitated. "There's no sign, 'For Sale,' or anything."

"Nobody's here to read signs."

"If you're that interested, let's look inside. All we know right now is, it has a fossil doorstone."

You looked at the ancient door. The sun-beaten wood shone orange, green and gray, like a living tree. The latch cast a delicate shadow. You knocked. The sound fell into stillness. Behind the door, listening silence breathed.

"Is there anyone there, said the Watcher!" You lifted the latch, and the door swung slowly back upon cobwebbed dimness. Facing us, steep, narrow stairs mounted against a central chimney. On the right opened the kitchen; small, timber-plastered, half lit by weed-screened windows, dominated by a huge iron range. "That would be the focal point of the house," you whispered, "especially in winter." It was cold, dust-blanketed, silent. But I imagined it polished, fire-crackling, with a teakettle bubbling on top; and the house came alive. It had been a home. Footsteps had creaked upstairs, thumped down the stairs, voices had risen around the range; angry voices, merry voices.

"Lynne, come look at this!" You were looking into the room on the other side. What intrigued you was the bay window. It had a broad window seat, which opened to reveal moldy blankets, wormy children's books. You shrugged, closed the lid, and knelt on it. "Look. They could see all the way to the hilltop."

"The woods are recent?"

"Oh, yes. The railroad killed the farms, didn't you know that? Railroads and taxes and public health. This country used to be all open fields." I hadn't known. I had thought we were wandering in the forest primeval.

Slowly, in a state of happy, leisured excitement, we explored the front rooms. You dusted the living-room secretary with your handkerchief; wandered across the front hall past the broad stairs and chimney, and tested the folding doors beyond. Creaking, they opened upon a stuffy little room. Afternoon light fell here, gilding a potbellied stove by the chimney. Like a veiled statue, an amorphous piece took up half the back wall. You showed me how it opened, folding back lids and dusting to resurrect the keyboard. I pushed down silent key after silent key. "Did they take the strings out?"

"It's an organ. You pump." You pressed floor pedals. Abruptly, the thing wailed. Abashed, we listened as silence closed in slowly. The sound of footsteps upstairs would not have surprised us, doors opening, a startled voice. Watching each other across the dusty organ, we admitted that we still did not feel alone.

"I suppose," you considered aloud, "The owner will want to move all this." You were enchanted. I was beginning to see possibilities. I thought that Neal would never come here. This was a world away from Neal, from the City and the Bomb. My own work could flourish here. I saw myself drawing, painting, etching, in a world of endless inspiration. Art could grow on this landscape, like one of those moon-mushrooms on a dead tree; an extension of nature. Love could grow here. The house was a compost of love. That was the presence in the house, now I recognized it: an aggregate of love.

But the old lady did not want the parlor organ. "Your children will enjoy it." (Prophetic doom!) And as for the little stove, "I'd have to hire a full-time sawyer to keep up with it!" (I thought, myself, it would make a nice planter.) All she took with her was the child's sampler from the front bedroom. It was a wretched thing. Even I, with absolutely no interest in

handicraft, could do better. It was an alphabet, I remember, faded blue and red, the letters stumbling and
reeling. The signature, NELLIE BEN, was drunken.
But it had a quaint frame, hand-carved, studded with
tiny cones. It breathed the innocence that invades the
taut mind like a sudden scent of balsam.

Maybe that was an omen. Maybe, smelling that
faint, fleeting scent of Innocence, I should have
known "This is not for us."

The house lived its own life. Coming in the front
door under the wines, I never felt I was coming *home*.
I had more the sensation of the bold visitor who
poked her head in the door and shouts, "Anybody
home?" Sitting on the back doorstone, watching the
evening light fade, I felt like an imposter; or an ac-
tress, playing to an imaginary audience. Quite des-
perately — sometimes — I wanted to be real in this
role; to fit easily into the life and expectations of the
house.

One hot Saturday I took the kids grocery shopping
in Northampton. Wearily I pushed the cart up and
down the aisles through crowds of Saturday shoppers;
it was like driving in traffic. Which is the better bar-
gain, six ounces for thirty-five or eight for forty-five,
quick, before the big woman in curlers bumps you?
Gwen hung onto the cart yelling, "Mommie, buy
Sweet Pops! Mommie, buy Sweet Pops!" I parked the
cart and Chris on Candy Street and hunted up and
down Cereal Street for Sweet Pops. When I returned,
Chris was curled up in the cart munching a Hershey
bar. I had parked unwisely.

I stood a long time at the cash register, exhausted,
hot and angry. The woman ahead of me shopped
once a month. Chris went to sleep, curled up on the
potatoes; Gwen grabbed an empty cart and zoomed
it up and down the crowded aisles.

At the next checkout waited a huge black woman.
She rested her bulk against the counter and talked
softly with two small boys, one black, one white. Her

round, relaxed face, her slow voice, beguiled me. She conversed with the toddlers as with equals; courteously, with interest, as though she delighted in their company and in the prospect of spending a long summer day with them; a prospect that horrified me, second-hand! It came to me that this huge, placid woman loved the kids. They did not send her screaming up the wall. She gave herself calmly to the kids, to the day, to the hot wait at the cash register. I scented balsam.

I know nothing of prayer. (One of these dreadful days Gwen is going to ask me about school prayers. This God person, did he really make the world? And I am going to tell her the truth. This is one of my nightmares.) But at the cash register I almost prayed. "If I could be like that black woman! If I could belong in our house!" For she would have belonged there.

I am nothing like her. I am tense, impatient, desirous. I want. As Gwen wants Sweet Pops, so I want to be Myself, the self with sharp edges. You used to joke about my coloring: "Red hair, hot temper." But I felt real anger, real frustration. Those cries of "Mommeeee" that tore me from my easel roused fury, imperfectly masked as solicitude. And your endless demands — *"When* are you taking the laundry in? Where is my new shirt? Hell, under the socks, all rumpled!"

There is nothing so boring, so crazifying, as housework; what women's magazines glamorize as "homemaking." You polish, you buff and wax and mop, you straighten and sort, you hunt spiders and moths through dark closets and sticky drawers. Next day, week, month, year, you do it again. Suppose in the meantime the house burns down? You see this in the papers every morning over coffee. Some dwelling-box has gone up in flames, with all its polishes and waxes, elbow grease and stitchery. Some woman's seven-day job has been reduced to cinders. I wonder, is she sorrowful? Does she mourn the sunlit hours wasted, spent inside the box cherishing ephemeral objects? Or does she possibly, secretly, rejoice?

I would stand in the dining-room doorway, looking at floor and window seat littered, table crumby and spilled-on, curtains drooping dustily; and a weird exhaustion would take me, so that I had to sit down. At first I thought I was sick. Words like "heart" and "blood pressure" flashed in my brain. But I despise hypochondria. I knew what the trouble was. "Is this trip really necessary?" I would ask myself as I sank into stupor.

I discovered two sure-fire cures; a bloody mary, and my easel.

Constant visions swarmed. In the early mornings I stood on the doorstone, watching the near hill take on form, meaning and color as my bit of earth met the sun. I watched the kids playing under the yard maple, hot light striking through cool leaves to pattern soft faces. All day the shadowed forest whispered mysteries; and on certain nights moonlight so silvered our room I could not sleep for watching its dreamy splendor. I thought, "If I can't paint here and now, I'd better learn shorthand!"

Canvas after canvas I stretched, blocked, underpainted. But at the dreaded cry of "Mommeeee!" I would leap away from the easel, as thought it were some embarrassing, secret habit I had. "Mommee, Gwen's got a snake, she's scaring me!" "Mommee, Chris piddled in the dragon tracks!"

So I tried watercolor. Watercolor is fast. You concentrate for an hour and it is finished, for good or ill. If for good, you hang it and marvel at it. "Did I do *that?*" For the geyser of inspiration has sunk underground again, and you have forgotten its power. If for ill, you crumple the painting.

Most of mine I crumpled. A few I hung in the barn, high out of reach of grubby paws. But two things troubled me about these relative successes.

They were far from avant-garde; in fact, they had old-fashioned, overt content. Secondly, the content was always the same. I was obsessed. Was it guilt? I wondered. Or was it some unconscious wisdom? Was I trying to tell myself something?

There was one of Gwen, swinging from a maple branch. There was one of Chris, "reading" on the window seat, framed in sunset. In one picture an unknown child ran, as graceful as some wild thing that lopes acoss the road in front of your headlights. When the yard shivered with angry children's voices I would retreat to the barn and stand looking up at these sunny, silent children. Out beyond the big doors bombs would boom, rockets screech; and between explosions the shocked air would hum with biting boredom. Almost happy, I would sink into the cool, green world of my own yearning creation.

Twice I have come slowly awake to dimness. I smelled anesthetic and flowers; and realized, with grateful wonder, the absence of pain. Came a starched nurse on cat feet, and placed a wrapped bundle beside me; "Baby Cambridge." I raised myself groggily, to look down upon a tiny face.

Its crumpled eyelids fluttered. Its rose-petal mouth twitched, sucked hope. An impossibly small hand waved free of the voluminous wrappings that smelled of cleanliness. Gingerly I touched the hand; it closed on my finger.

I spoke silently, for the nurse stood by. I felt that somehow, I was heard. This befogged, shocked creature, abruptly hauled out of the sea into air, seemed unaccountably communicado. Out of its roving, misty eye looked some wise mystery. You understand, I was none too clear myself. I was so unclear that I said to this bundle of problems, "Don't you worry. I'm going to do right by you. I'm going to be the best Mommie you ever had." And for a moment the vague, watery eyes seemed to focus on my face.

Even then — certainly the second time — I must

have had a suspicion that this promise would not be easily kept. It was like marriage, but irrevocable. If I walk out on you, tear up our treaty, you will not lie and kick and cry and stare at the wall and die. My commitment to you — while heavy enough — is limited. But to this new commitment I found no limitations.

While the babies were tiny it was all right. While they were soft and wordless, I not only wanted and intended to do right by them, I felt like it, too. Away from them I was uneasy. No painting, I thought, no job could seem as urgently important as these whimpering, squirming creatures — no matter what the demographers hissed, gathered like poisonous serpents at the nursery door. So what if there *were* too many people on the earth? Of all the people there were, these two were obviously the most important! And besides, who could take the demographers seriously, with Stalin balancing his Bomb? We were asked to worry about too many contradictions. One moment we were told we'd be bombed off the face of the earth; next moment, that we would populate ourselves to extinction. In the end, on the pretext of extreme busyness, I stopped reading intellectual magazines.

Meanwhile, individual life pulsed in those tiny bodies. It pushed and fountained and sprouted. Like saplings, they reached and shoved, straining for the sun. I felt their wriggling toes like roots, squirming into my lap. Stretching over my shoulder they crowed to the world, flinging eager hands to grasp at shadows or distant, flying birds. Their life-greed was limitless. Like sapped and tired earth, I soured.

Exhausted, I ran about after them, angrily trying to protect them from themselves. Dreadfully it dawned on me; milk and maternal instinct dry up; responsibility remains. These headstrong, life-drunk beings, devoid of both reason and instinct, were at my mercy.

I told myself, "I will not let them kill themselves." I shut my easel in the closet. And when Chris fell into the old water tank in the pantry, I called Flower

Brothers and had the damned thing yanked. I had always worried about it.

This was the one fly in the ointment, that day we wandered together through the empty house, and listened to its silences.

"Jeff," I said in the upstairs hall, "these are all bedrooms!"

"Naturally." Delighted, you examined the front south bedroom; canted ceiling, flowered paper, tilting floor.

"Jeff, there isn't any bathroom!"

"Oh." You glanced back over your shoulder; annoyance clouded your pale-blue eyes. "I saw a door down in the kitchen. That may be it."

Carefully, we descended the steep backstairs — "Eighteenth-century, believe it!" — back to the kitchen.

"Jeff! There isn't any sink!"

"Maybe back here . . ."

You showed me the pantry door. After some fighting with the frozen bolt you got it open; and the burble of water greeted us. There it was, the glorious Gravity Flow, of which owner and agent made so much. Quite simply, a stream was piped in one wall and out the other, with an open tank in the middle.

"My God!" I didn't believe it. "This isn't the water supply!"

"This is it!" Childishly, you dabbled your hands, even drank a little, disregarding my muttered warnings.

"And what," I demanded to know, "About the bathroom?"

"Oh, that will be a backhouse."

It was, by God! It was!

For you, the climax was capped. After all, you didn't have to live there all summer; only weekends.

I agreed to live there all summer. I thought I could paint there. I thought love could grow there; for the house was full of love, as a well is full of water. I feared to drown. And I thought your pal Neal would never come there.

He came the first weekend.

"Had the devil's own time finding you," he complained cheerfully, worming out of his foreign bug. "Nobody knows who you are, yet."

You giggled that hateful giggle you saved for Neal. "They're not going to, either! We have no intention of being known to the Natives! How *did* you find us?"

"Asked at the post office. Nobody there ever heard of Cambridge." (I rectified that on Monday.) "I described the place, going by what you'd told me; and finally this bearded old-timer squawks, "Ayah! He means the *Bennett* place!" And right away they were all over me with a hundred ways to get here; shorter ways, easier ways, pretty ways. I took the historic way, myself. Well. Let's have a look."

Like you, Neal paled with delight. He exclaimed joyously over everything. The fossil tracks bugged his eyes. The Gravity Flow produced his camera. Next morning he was up at sunrise, tiptoeing about the dewy yard shooting birds, flowers, stone walls.

"Flowers with stones," he explained at breakfast, "make for mystery." Almost gravely he added, "You've got a ghost, you know."

Neal could be very charming. I hated him, even then. I would have been pleased to hear of his sudden, painless demise. Yet I couldn't help responding to his charm almost as you did, or as the kids did, later. I smiled and handed over his third coffee. "So long as it doesn't creep about at night," I said.

I swear, he blushed! But he countered slyly, "Ah, you must provide chamber pots. Willow Pattern."

He crept about at night a great deal. Sleepless on a moonlit night I would stand at our window and watch him pace the lawn like a restless shadow. Sometimes he would pause, and look up at our window. Then I would draw back into shadow, as though *I* were the spy!

Those were the nights — and more and more frequently they came — when you and I didn't make it. "I'm tired," you would say.

Exasperated at first, I might protest. "How can you be tired, just from sitting in a lawn chair and holding up a drink?"

You would shrug. The bedsprings registered our mutual withdrawal. Later, there would be Neal's white face on the lawn, upturned to the window.

We went to Neal's one-man show in the City, and there was a sparkling, gleaming shot of our Gravity Flow system emptying into the tank. It was captioned, "From the Mountain." But then Chris fell into the water tank. Gwen's shrieks brought me bounding from my newly resurrected easel. I had just contracted to illustrate a dinosaur book — you wouldn't get me a job, I actually had to contact a rival agent — and I had money. Without consulting you, I called Flower Brothers in Winterfield. Before you and Neal returned, the Gravity Flow was gone, the artesian well dug, and the bathroom was taking shape in the erstwhile pantry.

You leaned in the door, looking; very cold, very distant. Neal drooped his long nose over your shoulder, and smiled at me from under his fair, flopping bangs. "Actually, Jeff, it's not so bad. To tell the truth it was kind of cold on the toes, tripping to the backhouse in the wee hours!"

From that beginning I went on. Every weekend you come home you found more change. I got Mr. Little from the Center to paint the house. He came with a gang of boys — sons, nephews, daughters' boyfriends — and when you came back the house was white. "I wasn't sure I was home," you said, wearily stomping up the bank. By the next weekend the shutters were back on, mended and painted green; and the lawn was rolled and seeded.

The Bennett place entered a new incarnation. Seen from the dirt road, it now looked quite respectable. Gray maple-shadows painted its white clapboards. Little, wavery window panes winked in the sun. (True, the rooftree sagged, and the south end bulged.) Neal took pictures of it from different angles, some from the road, some from the back hill, showing the ell; "in case you ever want to sell it; or for your album." He laid them out on the kitchen table, and we stooped over them. You said brightly, "Hey! Let's invite the mothers!"

We had never yet invited either mother to visit. We had felt, and told each other, "They wouldn't understand." The isolation would bother them, the backhouse, the abandoned, rustic effect you loved.

"Sure," I agreed indifferently. "Why not? Ask your mother for Labor Day." I felt the house looking over my shoulder and rejecting its new image. "That's not Me," said the house; not for the first time.

I sensed the house as a personality. Especially when I worked at night, trying to catch up on my wasted day, the house breathed down my neck. Drinking midnight coffee at the kitchen table, staring across the hall to the dining-room door, I half expected to see it drift slowly open, as in a dream. A presence weighted the indoor air. I was too much alone.

Perhaps to strike back at this ghostly presence, the following summer I undertook *indoor* renovations. Neal had remarked on the absence of fireplaces. "A house simply isn't a home without a fireplace; flames you can sit and look into, you know. You've got two chimneys; there must be fireplaces, boarded up." He tapped slender knuckles behind the kitchen range, made a face, and cradled his bruised hand.

I called Flower Brothers back. Burly men in overalls, spattered with paint and grease, came and tapped, measured and drilled. They reported fireplaces concealed in kitchen and dining room; none in the front rooms. They went off, leaving one bent, elderly Flower looking the kitchen chimney up and down, thoughtfully rubbing his hands on his overalls.

Eban Flower had hands like screwdrivers. I have heard it said that Eban could drive a nail with his fist, and I almost believe it. Matter-of-factly he shoved the iron range aside — I cooked on the little gas stove, of course — and went at the boarded-up chimney. The first day he ripped out six feet of wall, exposing very rough plaster — "horsehair" — and crumbling laths.

"Look at this stuff!" he commanded as I wandered past, hunting an ashtray; obedient, I stopped dead, cigarette dripping ash.

Eban made me see the crumbs and splinters, the dusty, papery effect of the whole mess. "You want to be mighty careful with an old house like this one. See that insulation? Newspaper! See that stick, how dry? You could light your cigarette with that! Half the old houses in town burned down, you know."

"Oh?"

"Ayah, they did! Not more'n ten houses this old left in town. I'm telling you, ma'am."

"I see."

The kids watched, enthralled. Eban had this in common with the black woman whose image still haunted me reproachfully: kids did not drive him up the wall. Good-naturedly, between puffs on the corncob pipe clenched in his brown teeth, he taught them the names of his hundred tools and their uses; and where they belonged in his toolbox. He made them apprentices. Chris soon tired and returned to his picture books. But Gwen spent a deliriously happy week handing Eban tools, returning them, and watching the careful, precise demolition of the kitchen wall.

"Mommie!" She came trotting to me, where I stood at my easel in the dining-room. "Mommie, we've got a *secret compartment!*"

Sighing, I let her haul me back to the kitchen. The secret compartment was a hole behind a loose brick. Eban drew forth brittle, dust-veiled objects. One of these turned out to be a wad of papers, which broke and crumbled at a touch. Letters. A shaky hand, either decrepit or unlettered, had written across the paper, then turned it and written across again; so that the second lines effectively canceled out the first. I barely made out the words: "Ohio, farm, Father." I set the wad aside, not wanting to dump it in the trash under Eban's grave eyes. He seemed so proud of his find!

The other object was "Noah Stone His Horne"; an authentic, genuine, antique, yellowed powder horn. Eban handled this reverently, turning it gently in his rough hands, interpreting the crude, scratched drawings for us. "This Noah Stone was an Indian fighter," he told open-mouthed Gwen. Craning to look over his shoulder, I saw a stick-man, ax in hand, creeping up behind another, oblivious stick-man in a triangular hat.

"Here?" Gwen squeaked. "Did he fight Indians *here?*"

"Oh, I wouldn't think that. Never heard of Indians around here. Look at this, now; interestin'." He turned the horn to show a lean, swaying stick-man in a triangle. With a jagged spear this unfortunate held at bay some bristling beast. "He killed a bear with a stick. No, see the tail. Must be a wolf."

"She," Gwen said positively.

"Um?"

"Dress." Gwen traced the triangle around the feeble figure.

"Well, well. Could be. Wouldn't surprise me none." Nodding, Eban blew a cloud of smoke over the horn; but I had seen that Gwen was right. Noah Stone may have been a great Indian fighter, but he was no artist.Yet I could clearly see the skirt in the faltering triangle.

"Now as to this," Eban mumbled — a rectangle gave off sunrays — "as to this, I give up."

"Me too." Gwen shrugged it off. She wanted to see the Indian again.

Later, alone in the dining room, I laid the horn between my hands on the table. Eban was sweeping up in the kitchen, Gwen had deserted him for the parlor organ. Even two rooms away, her one-fingered rendition scraped the nerves.

"Ain't that tune a weddin' march?" I heard Eban ask Chris. I could imagine Chris staring back at him, his wide eyes friendly and uncomprehending. "Sounds more like a funeral march from here!"

Noah Stone lived in a man's world. They say we do today, but this is nonsense. I can do what you can do. If I am stuck here, cooking and wiping noses and refereeing, it's my own fault. One bright, June morning, in the presence of my mother's roses and fifty guests, and to that same moronic tune that Gwen sent wailing through the house, I made you an impossible promise. That folly was my own. Today, I might have been an illustrator, agent, receptionist — any number of things. The City is nearly as open to me as to you.

But Noah Stone's drawings reflected a different world entirely. A cold breeze seemed to blow from the horn into my hands. Perhaps there was, in that cold air, a faint scent of balsam. But there was more of dirty leather and woodsmoke. I saw that world black-and-white, like a crude woodcut. Was it Noah's presence I felt in the house, silent, inimical? Was it the thin woman who killed the bear with a stick? Did I feel her cold scorn? The scratched symbols merged with Wagner to send shivers up my neck. I actually shuddered, and glanced around the empty dining room.

"My God! I really am too much alone! At this speed I'll end up playing Emily May in the lilacs!"

My mother said the same. "You're too much alone, Lynne. I haven't seen a soul but the milkman and the handyman since I came."

She was ironing sheets in the dining room while I pretended to paint. With her there, I couldn't really paint; I couldn't concentrate. But it was an excuse for not helping her sort socks, wax floors, or iron.

The steam iron flashed in afternoon sunlight. The board stood in the bay window, beside a window seat piled high with shirts, sheets, handkerchiefs, pillow cases, even the kids' jeans. Slim and sprightly in crisp blouse and slacks, Mother kept her back to me; I saw only her curly hair, dyed a lively red; the nape of her bowed neck; and the milky sheen of her elbow sweeping back and forth across the board. A nimbus of gold dust floated around her. She could not see this, of course, it was only visible from my angle.

"That's no handyman," I said absently, watching the lovely whirl of dust. "That's Mr. Flower. I introduced you." Ripping sounds in the kitchen were followed by Gwen's squeals. "Oh God, I hope he hasn't made some new historical discovery!"

"If you're not *interested,* Lynne, why are you doing this?"

Mother's back being squarely turned made talking possible.

"For Jefferson."

She thumped down the iron, shook out a sheet. "The little I saw of him Sunday, he didn't seem that crazy about it."

"He doesn't like the mess. But he'll love it when it's done. We're going to have an authentic eighteenth-century farmhouse!"

"Dandy." I knew well how the hidden lips pursed! "But you don't live in the eighteenth century, God help you; you live in the twentieth. Don't you think . . ." Mother bowed farther over the board, hunched her slim shoulders. Was *she* having trouble talking to *me?* Was I "difficult"?

"Do you think Jefferson will spend more time here when it's done?"

"It's the Agency, Mom."

"Well, then. Do you think you might want to stay in the City more, spend more time with *him?*"

"Kids need a solid home." Astonished, I heard my voice shake.

Abruptly, she changed tack. "The children are too much alone, too. Haven't they any friends in the village?"

"Well, actually, the Natives . . . no."

"What do the Natives do for whoopla?"

"Mothers' Club. Grange. Church." My eloquent shrug was lost on Mother's back.

"Sounds pleasant." (Mother was serious.) "I bet they have a garden club. Did I tell you Honor Beadle got second prize with those Golden Hinds I gave her?"

We did not talk again. You understand, we exchanged phrases and sentences of more and less import. But we were careful not to touch nerve.

On the last morning of her visit Mother packed us and a picnic into her foreign bug, and we drove out to the old Squire Winter farm. This is the highest, most isolated spot in isolated Winterfield. We sat in the shade of an apple tree that bowed like a haggard ballet dancer, fingers combing the grass. We looked down and across a tumbling, rocky pasture to where a dip of forest hid the road. Beyond was a smaller mountain, called Nellie's Knoll, with the Bennett place tucked into its far side; and the distant spires of Northampton gleamed, apparently, from a sea of forest.

"Wanna go home," Gwen declared, chomping the end of the last ham sandwich. "I reckon Eban's near about done." She had picked up his lingo, along with his habit of rubbing hands on pants. If she had got hold of a corncob pipe she would have smoked it.

"Let's pause a while," Mother suggested calmly, "and enjoy the view." Mother is much more relaxed, and therefore authoritative, with my kids than she was with me. Gwen acquiesced. But she hung about restlessly, listening in. Chris curled down between two apple roots and went to sleep. I wished I had brought my sketch pad!

"I wonder if this view will be here to see in another ten years," Mother mused. I thought she referred to Bombs; for a moment the whole ugly world came swarming toward us through the summer sky. But she went on, "Things move so fast, these days, I can see some ideal spots down there for development."

Oh. That was all! "You expect us to be a Northampton suburb in ten years?"

"The way the population is exploding, it's bound to come." Mother glanced up against the light, at listening Gwen. I poured us each a thimble from my shot flask. She accepted hers reluctantly. "A bit early for this."

That word *population* strikes me as dirty. It turns up more and more frequently in magazines, even on the radio. Somebody wants me to feel *guilty* about having kids, for Christ's sake! Somebody wants me to know my kids aren't worth having, the world would be better off without them. I turn the radio off when I hear that word, in case the kids might hear, and get some vague inkling that the world doesn't want them.

Mother felt the same way, I could see it in her guilty, upward glance. That tipped Gwen off. Instantly she asked, "What's population?"

"People, dear. Numbers of people. See those asters down there? Would you like to pick some for . . . for the dining-room table?"

But that didn't work. We finished our drinks, carefully packed the picnic refuse, and drove home without discussing the population thing.

Next day you came back, with Neal.

So I was glad Mother had left early. Some things — quite a lot of things — Mother doesn't know. It would be awful to live next door, like the Natives, and have Mother Know All.

She kissed me goodbye and said, "I like your home-perm."

I assured her, "In the fall I get it done right. This is just for here."

As our breaths mingled, I realized that I didn't know very much about Mother, either. I didn't know what she would do next morning, for instance; to what plan of action she would wake in her silent garden apartment. Mother had given her life to my father, and to me. Now that he is dead and I am five hundred miles away, where does that leave Mother?

I don't know. I don't want to know. I can't afford to know.

Neal exclaimed wildly over the uncovered eighteenth-century fireplace. "Now you want herbs hanging from the beams! And a brass pot and a settle! Oh yes, a settle on the hearthstone!"

The hearthstone was immense. Gwen looked at it indifferently — no baby dinosaur had walked across it. I touched it uneasily with a sneakered toe. It smelled of the alien, hostile eighteenth century. "Now, a spinning wheel" — Neal was rhapsodizing — "well, perhaps not. You want to avoid the obviously fake."

The obviously fake. By this time, you and I going to bed together was obviously fake. It was almost all right by me. My hungers had always been blunted by anxiety. Neither condom nor diaphragm had worked, after all! No matter what the women's magazines insist, with their astonishing new freedom — "sex" has become a respectable word, perfectly printable — no matter what psychologists expound, I do not believe women will ever accept lovemaking as a harmless sport, unless a foolproof method is found.

But as I was concerned with our fast-deteriorating relationship I made a last, tentative advance.

You leaped up, hastily pulled on your robe. The nights were chilly, even in August.

"Look," you said, "it's no good. It's just no good." I lay and watched you. Moonlight silvered the edge of the robe, a patch of your hair. I felt sorry for you. In a way, I have always felt sorry for men.

"It's temporary," I assured you, and myself.

"I don't know about that." You fumbled in the robe for a cigarette.

"Jeff. Is something eating you?"

"Is something eating me? My God!" You fished up a cig, dug farther for a match. "You don't know the pressures, you have no idea! Rat race. Office rent, taxes, apartment rent, insurance — two kids! You know what private schools are going to cost? No, you don't know — you live in a dreamworld out here! Do you even know there's a *war* on, for Christ's sake?"

I didn't try to sort this out. One element had caught my attention. Now I was angry, and I sat up and swung my feet over the side. "And *why* do I live in a dreamworld here? *Who* didn't want me to work? *Who* wanted a full-time wife-mother?"

"Okay. Keep it down." You found and struck a match. Quick yellow flame marred the moonlight. "It's partly my fault, I know it. I tell you, sometimes I think . . . I think I'm not cut out for this."

"You get the best end!"

"You mean, I get to pay the bills?"

"I mean you get to work! You go where you want, do what you want. I'm the one stuck out here with a couple of whiny brats!"

"In the fall — "

"In the fall I'm stuck in the apartment with a couple of whiny brats." Self-pity jarred my voice. Self-disgust silenced me. I was relieved, almost cheered, when you sat down by me and proffered the pack. But I shook my head.

You spoke, then, from a surprising new angle. "You've done a great job here. Doesn't look like the same place. Real Estate's up."

It was like a sharp, light blow. "You want to sell?"

"Not tomorrow, no."

"Later on, it might look different."

"That's what I tell myself."

Then I took a cigarette. We inhaled together, side by side on the rumpled bed. When I touched your hand you let it lie. I reminded you, "This is a long-term thing. We're bound to have ups and downs."

"Time for an up."

Later you lay down, pulled up the sheet and began heavy breathing. I couldn't tell if it was genuine. I felt a headache coming on, and a twitchiness. "Better get an aspirin, maybe a nightcap." Stealing past the window, I paused to look out over the porch roof, down the bank.

Moonlight washed the grass. Moonlight tipped the lilac leaves. Below, the massed bushes were a thicket of darkness.

In the midst of that thicket stands an old hitching stone. The kids discovered it buried in growth while they were playing Emily May. It is tall and lean, and twists slightly sideways, as though yielding to the top-heavy weight of its iron ring. I thought someone had cleared the thicket, and I was looking at that hitching stone standing clear in the moonlight.

Then it flickered, a small, white twitch. I saw a thin face turned upward, staring with sorrowful, shadowed eyes at our window. Neal was out, prowling the night.

Sorrowful, top-heavy. I had never realized Neal before. Looking down through the uncertain, distorting glass, I hated my own isolation. I go around armed with helmet and shield. Sometimes I make an effort to see past someone else's visor — yours, or the kids', or Mother's. But the effort is strenuous. I am glad to retreat into myself, and snap my own visor shut. I had seen Neal only as an armed enemy; never as a fellow creature, a center of private unhappiness.

For the first time I watched Neal's vague, moon-shimmered figure without hate, without anger. Even while I watched I heard the stealthy click of his door, and his creak on the front stairs.

Confused, I glanced back at you. You were an inert bunch of sheet. Was one of the kids out there, sleepwalking? I looked back to the lilacs. That patch of moonlight was empty.

With Neal patrolling the yard, I did not want to turn on the kitchen light and pour a nightcap. I decided to wait for his sneaking return. But I did go, barefoot, shivering, to look in on the kids.

Moonlight flooded the bunk beds. I picked my way cautiously across the floor, squelching gum and paste and a picture book. On the top bunk Gwen lay, bare and spread-eagled, grinding her teeth. I lifted the sheet over her very gently, for Gwen could jerk awake in an instant. Chris, curled up like a baby porcupine, snored softly.

Nobody was out sleepwalking.

In the morning the two of you went away. And while the kids played in the lilacs, I sketched my unexpected Vision. Straight she stood beside the massive tree, that magnificent old lady. She looked up out of the sketch, through the fall of light. Her gaze was serene as mine was nervous, her mind as single as mine was torn. Like Athena, she was born fully mature, from a headache. And I hung the sketch in the barn and gazed at it, for healing.

I set up my easel in the barn, for this time I meant business. The kids would be perfectly safe moseying around outside. I could hear their squawks. At first I thought I could ignore them. My attention was firmly centered upon the canvas before me.

This was the largest sheet of white canvas I had ever faced. I hurled myself at it, into it, with the fury of inspiration. From the moment the Vision emerged from darkness into mental daylight, I knew I could paint it. The image vibrated certainty. Its own violent energy precluded any possibility of failure. And I, who usually sketch and resketch, paint and overpaint with trembling humility, approached this canvas with calm assurance. I knew I had only to mix paint and apply.

I dabbed the number 10 brush on the gray-green which would be the prevailing undertone, and leaned forward.

"I'll explode you!" Gwen roared just outside. "You'll explode POW!"

"Go on!" Chris was complacent. "I'm people."

"That's why you'll explode, you ass! People explode!"

Over my shoulder the dangling light bulb seemed to

tremble. The air hissed. Brush almost on canvas, I hesitated.

"See this here thing?" Gwen's softer voice was menacing. "See this thing came from outer space. It's a . . . a meety . . . it fell outta the sky. It'll explode you good, Buddy!"

Chris said calmly, "Get outta my way."

His nonchalance drove Gwen over the edge. I felt it happen, like a lightning-strike. Then followed a rustling rush, a screech.

Slowly I stepped back from the canvas. Carefully I laid down the charged brush. Then I ran to the door. Already contrite, Gwen was lifting Chris onto shaky legs. The object she had used to explode him lay just behind her, jagged point up.

"Gwen, don't step back."

She did.

Later I found that the point had neatly sliced her sneaker sole in half. At the moment I was looking for blood, and mightily relieved to find none. A cut from that ragged, rusty point would have meant a trip to Northampton Hospital, and no mistake!

"It isn't a meety is it?" Chris asked, holding his bruised head.

"A meteor? Of course not." I turned it over, wondering. It was long and sharp and iron, rust-eaten beyond shape.

"It isn't!" he told Gwen spitefully. "You said it was a meety, and it isn't!"

"It must be a tool." Or a weapon. "Where did it come from, Gwen?"

She nodded uphill, past the barn. "I found it, Mommie. It's mine."

"Not if you use it to hit people." I carried it into the barn and stashed it on a high shelf. I thought you might want to see it. (I didn't know time was growing short.) Neal had taught me well that on a damned historic site like this, one throws away no trash. Trash can easily turn out to be priceless antiques.

Chris was unhurt. But he whined about feeling dizzy all day, and I had to keep a fracture watch.

All day the Vision stood in my mind, radiant, demanding. At ten o'clock, after six glasses of water, four trips to the bathroom, and a story twice repeated, the kids were finally asleep. I tiptoed downstairs, eased myself out the back door, and ran for the barn.

The last advice Mother ever dared give me — and the best — was "Never leave little children alone in the house." Every day you hear it on the radio: some disaster, which occurred while Father was at work and Mother shopping; or while Mother had slipped next door for a coffee break; or the babysitter had sneaked out back with her boyfriend. Kids can set fire to a house, playing with matches; then they go hide in bed. Or they can turn the stove on, and crawl on top of it; or push the baby into the dryer and turn it on. The depth of my desperation shows clearly here. I left the house, and the kids sleeping; and worked in the barn, thirty yards away, all night.

Every so often I paused and stood in the barn doorway, watching the dark house, listening for frightened voices. Behind me the barn swam in the rich, heavy smell of oils. Turning back, I saw the painting afresh; growing, like a living being, according to plan. I was joy-dizzied.

For two, three nights I breathed oil, turpentine and coffee. Leaning in the doorway I listened to the cry of crickets in the cold grass. Sometimes an owl hooted eerily. The outdoor night was a new world to me. I forgot who I was and why I was watching the house. Stillness and cool dark engulfed me. The painting, glowing on its easel under the bulb, was my reality.

I think it was last Thursday night when I looked across cricket country — and saw a light! I gasped; and remembered my identity. I was the mother of Gwen and Chris. "Christ, they'll be scared!" I ran, stumbling, down across the lawn.

The light shone from the dining-room window. I

spied on tiptoe. It was a soft light, mild, like the glow of an oil lamp. Astonished, I stared at the bowed back of a plump woman, seated at the table, head slumped below shoulders. An aura of cold despair seemed to weigh her down.

In another breath I recognized the scene. Sometime during the drugged day I had dumped a load of dirty laundry on the chair, overflowing the table. A gauzy curtain had fallen across the lampshade. I must have left the light on, myself, in my joyful rush to the barn. "Hell!" I thought, shocked. "It could have fired the house!"

I went in and listened up the stairs for a few moments. No sound. Intensely relieved, I turned off the light — the gauze was hot — and bounded back to the barn, where my old lady stood now triumphant, dowdily regal. Her posture was erect, yet relaxed. The face was still a blur; but the gnarled, folded fingers had been perfected.

In the misty morning I meandered back to the house. The painting was vivid before my eyes, more real than the long grass, cricket-rustled. From the house came a moaning wail; Gwen's wedding march, so early?

"I'm always up early," she assured me. "I always watch you come back. Listen, Mommie." She repeated the performance, one forefinger crushing down the keys, both feet pumping madly. I yawned, and abandoned tact.

"It doesn't sound like Wagner to me."

" 'Course it doesn't! It's a wedding march!" It droned on all day, a reminder of something; a warning.

As the long, agonizingly dull day waned, my spirits rose. I woke up, stretched, drank coffee, took No-Doz. Inside my eyes stood the luminous Vision. "Tonight," I promised her, "we finish!"

But in late afternoon came the two of you.

Chris bumbled down the bank, chubby arms outstretched. "Daddy-Daddy-Daddy!" Gwen followed

more slowly. She kept glancing from me to you, and
back. You held out your arms to Chris; even as he
flung himself into them, your face changed. "Hell's
bells, boy! I thought we had plumbing!"

Neal slid out of the car. Nervously, he glanced
from you to me.

You kissed the top of Chris's curls and set him
down very firmly, as though he were a dirty-pawed
puppy. To me you said, fairly pleasantly, "What the
hell have you been doing?"

I began to understand. I did not exactly *see,* I *saw*
nothing but the Vision in my head. But I realized we
must all be remarkably unkempt. No one had had a
bath in a week. I had lost track of hair- and tooth-
brushes.

I explained. "I've been working."

You went past me, into the house. I heard curses,
stampings around. I sat down on the grass and contemplated my Vision.

Later, Neal came to me and said gently, "Go get
dolled up, honey. We're eating in Northampton."

I made an empty-headed effort. "You're tired of
driving. Let me rustle something up."

Neal looked at me sadly. "Can you rustle up something besides Sweet Pops?"

Well after midnight I crept back to the easel. I
pulled the dangling string, and light burst. There stood
ancient tree and woman, side by side, light-drenched.
Roots and feet firmly met firm, dappled earth.
Branches reached to infinity. The folded hands had
no need to reach.

With the number 1 brush I went to work on the
face. So powerful was the force within, pushing to
materialize, I suffered not the slightest hesitation. The
brush dipped and dabbed, and expression merged,
swimming up out of the formless mass.

I stood back. The old lady looked out past me with
calm intelligence. Decision was in her face, and acceptance of decision. She decided all, she accepted

all. The very painting in which she stood was her decision. I laid the brush down.

The picture lightened, wet oil glistened. "Mommie."

I reached up, pulled the cord. The painting stood up well to natural daylight.

Natural daylight? I looked around.

The great barn doors framed pale, green light. A small shadow leaned against the jamb. "Mommie. Chris wants his breakfast."

"So get it for him."

"No Sweet Pops. I never cooked bacon. Want me to?"

"God, no! Get Daddy to cook."

"He's still asleep."

That streak of highlight down the maple was too clean. It needed a bit of fuzzing. "What?"

"Daddy and Neal are still asleep." Did the young voice accuse? "They're snoring."

"I see."

The old lady watched, unsurprised; accepting.

"I'll come."

Companionably, we strolled down to the house. My slacks were wet to the knee. Gwen's small, bare feet were pink.

"Gwen, aren't your feet cold?"

"I like how the grass feels. And I like how turp smells. Let me carry it?" I gave her the can.

Approaching the house, I looked up at it affection-ately. Maple branches caressed the sagging rooftree. Sunlight glanced along it. Where the ell joined the front section the sag was worse, and there were shin-gles missing. The side of the house was in shadow; sunlight would be striking full upon the front, all the little window panes would be twinkling. I stepped up on the huge, fossiled doorstone and pulled open the screen door.

"Let's have the turp, Gwen."

"Hey, don't spill it!"

"I'm not spilling. I'm pouring. Where's Chris?"

Chris peeped around the kitchen door. His soft face

was jam-streaked. In his fist he gripped a soggy sandwich.

"Chris, you go outside. Get in my car. We're going for a ride."

He demurred. "Gotta go — "

"Never mind that. Get in the car, *now*."

"But I gotta — "

I grabbed his arm and yanked him outside, pushing Gwen ahead. "You kids get in the car, my car, and stay there."

"Okay, okay, keep your pants on." Gwen's green eyes narrowed, alert and frightened; which a moment before had been calm, with a sort of adult friendliness.

I watched the kids stumble uncertainly down the bank, Chris dripping jam, Gwen pausing to look back. Furiously I waved her on. "And *stay* there!" Gwen pushed Chris into the back seat of my car — loudly he lamented his squashed sandwich — and climbed in herself. *"Lock the door!"* I went back in the house and sprinkled. I laid a turpentine trail through the dining room, pausing at the bay window to drench the curtain hems. I crossed the hall and puddled the kitchen. (Now I was glad I never got around to putting down linoleum. Those wide, crumby boards would work wonders!) I dribbled through the pantry, and left the empty can where the trough used to be, just outside the bathroom door.

Then I went back through the kitchen to the hall, and shouted up the backstairs. "Jefferson Cambridge!"

I shouted over and over, till my voice went hoarse. At last bare feet flapped in the upstairs hall. Neal called sleepily, "Whassa matter?"

"Listen, Neal. You go out the front way, and quick!"

"Huh?"

"I'm telling you, get out the front door. The house is on fire."

Neal raised a startled cry. "Fire!"

You roared from bed, "Call the Volunteer —"

"Have you called —"

"Shut up, Neal." I was picking the matchbook out of my shirt pocket. "There's no time to call. You two get your butts outside before it blows."

Another boom from bed. *"The kids?"*

Neal, in treble. *"The kids?"*

"The kids are safe outside. Now, move it."

I went back to the dining room and approached the soaked curtains. Ceiling and stairs rumbled with your rushing escape. Briefly I remembered the old lady, safe in the barn thirty yards away. Half turned toward the open door, she would see at least the reflection of fire. Her complacent gaze would accept it.

I lit the match, stooped to the curtain. Flame caught, leaped, soared.

I walked leisurely through the living room, and went out through the front door you had left ajar. Morning sunshine flooded the porch, the bittersweet cast no cool shadow now. The two of you stood well out on the lawn, exclaiming, pointing to roof and windows, where no sign of fire yet appeared.

Walking out to you through dewy grass, I heard behind me the immensely satisfying roar of bursting light; of liberated, triumphant, self-intending light.

Finale

Stand up from the doorstone. Scrub with your shoe the covering, clinging mosses.

There is the track: a small, three-toed foot-mark, pressed in mud, preserved in stone. There is the next one, and the next. When the little dinosaur crossed here, did the spring flow?

Climb the hill once more. Pushing through thicket and brush, follow what may have been the tile pipe's trail up along a stone wall, past the crumbling sugar-house to the spring.

Stand on the brink of the shining pool; look down into mirrored sky. Look up at the cliff face, spray-splattered. Gleaming water springs from the rock, flings out and down the rock-face into a stone bowl, hammered by a thousand years of water, falling.

Flung into sunlight the water splashes into shadow. In all the shifting shade and sparkle the sober judgment of the eye is dazzled. A bayonet blade, glinting among stones, becomes a poised snake. A white flicker among leaves was a bird, departing. A child's soft face peers at you around the trunk of a white birch; it is only reflected water-light.

Bend to the hammered bowl. Kneel on wet rock and drink, scooping the water in your palm, holding back your hair with one hand.

Drink your fill. The waters rush endlessly down the rock, from earth to brief sunshine, to shadow, to earth.